A TOAST TO THE LORD

A TOAST TO THE LORD

A NOVEL

by

ROBIN JENKINS

LONDON
VICTOR GOLLANCZ LTD
1972

© Robin Jenkins 1972

ISBN 0 575 01464 4

For May

Printed in Great Britain by
Northumberland Press Ltd., Gateshead

The town of Ardhallow exists only in the imagination. Therefore all its inhabitants, and its institutions, including St Aidan's Church and the U.S.S. *Perseus*, are imaginary too.

PART ONE

ON A BRIGHT summer afternoon the ferry-boat *St Columba* was crossing the Firth of Clyde to the small resort of Ardhallow. Yachts' sails and gulls' wings gleamed whitely against the blue sky and sea, and houses against green hills.

Two young women were standing by the rail, their hair moving in the breeze. The small dark one looked up at her tall fair companion and whispered, with careful fervour: "Aren't we lucky, Dora?"

Eagerly then, yet with a sly amusement, she studied her friend's reaction.

Dora smiled: she looked moved by Agnes's humble gratitude, but also uneasy as if she thought it unjustified and therefore perhaps insincere. Poor Agnes, her smile said, so grateful and yet with nothing really to be grateful about.

Agnes's own smile subtly deepened. She knew so well that Dora pitied her and did not think her at all lucky: she knew far more intimately than Dora herself the reasons for that pity.

To begin with, she wasn't attractive like Dora. Her skin was blemished, her hair had dandruff, her legs were thick. She had worked hard to remove or mitigate these defects, but what she had not done and never would do was to ask the Lord's help: that was reserved for more important

7

things than physical attractiveness.

Because of her appearance, and of her devoutness, which made her in so many people's eyes look stupid, she had not got nearly so good a rating as Dora in the training college from which they were now returning for the last time, as certificated teachers. She would probably have to be content with some tiny inconvenient school among the hills, while lucky Dora would be given a post in Ardhallow itself.

Agnes's mother was always ill, blue-lipped and damp-haired. Dora's was peacefully dead, buried in St Aidan's kirkyard, under a gean tree that in spring was glorious with white blossom.

Agnes had no sweetheart. Dora was engaged to Edward Raitt, only son of John Raitt, owner of the biggest building business in the town, and the employer of Agnes's father, a joiner. Agnes did not like Edward Raitt: at school he had often teased her because of her piousness and her unangelic looks. A medical student, he considered himself casually a Christian, but Agnes knew there was in him the blankness that came from disbelief. He would never make a good doctor. He saw only his own desires, never the Lord's. True, he was handsome, with his curly hair and brown eyes; naked—and Agnes had often imagined him naked, as a kind of revenge—he was no doubt exciting; but that excitement would soon pass and he would be dull for the rest of his life.

Still, everybody else thought Dora fortunate to be engaged to him.

But Agnes's worst misfortune, in Dora's opinion, shared by almost the whole of Ardhallow, was her father, William Tolmie, leading member of the local branch of the Church of Christ the Master, which he had founded himself. In a town that called itself Christian and had six churches in use, Mr Tolmie was laughed at for what was called his bigotry and his reading of the Bible, from Genesis to

8

Revelation, to his family in the evenings. What they did not know, and what would have made them laugh more coarsely and cruelly, was that he lived in terror because the Lord had turned away from him. For over thirty-five years, since his acknowledgement at the age of ten of the Lord as his Saviour, Mr Tolmie had prayed, read the Bible, preached, and believed more than any other man in Scotland. He should have been rewarded with the Lord's shining approval; instead, there had been a long eclipse, until now only the darkness of rejection remained. That terrible judgement he had accepted without complaint.

By contrast, Dora's father, the Rev. Robert Plenderleith, minister of St Aidan's, which had the highest steeple and the biggest stipend of all the churches in the town, was surely foremost among the Lord's chosen. His face shone. Tall and robust, he had once played rugby for Scotland. He spoke in a fine ringing Scots voice, without any genteel affectation or slovenliness. All the best citizens worshipped under him, the bank managers, hotel owners, contractors, shopkeepers, the Rector of the High School, and even, now and then, the Captain of the U.S.S. *Perseus*, which lay anchored in Loch Hallow right under his manse windows, sometimes with its nurslings, the Polaris submarines, snuggled against it. Everyone knew that Mr Plenderleith, as a sincere follower of Christ, could not quite bring himself to bless the H-bombs within his parish so to speak, but since he kept his scruples to himself and never uttered them in his pulpit, they were not held against him; indeed, his parishioners were rather pleased that their minister on all their behalfs kept one foot, however gingerly, in Christ's camp.

When his wife had died his grief had been nobly sustained. Agnes, then thirteen, had sneaked into St Aidan's to admire it. At that time Mr Plenderleith, with his lovely voice and small mouth, had often appeared in her masturbatory day-dreams. Recently, however, he had

9

become engaged to Elizabeth Greenloaning, the wealthiest woman in Ardhallow, and proprietrix of the biggest hotel. Except for a few disgruntled widows in his congregation everybody said that Elizabeth would make an excellent wife and stepmother, being sympathetic, intelligent, sensitive, and efficient.

Agnes did not like Elizabeth Greenloaning. This was wrong of her. Hatred was only permissible if the Lord demanded or suggested it. In Elizabeth's case He had not done so, as He had in Edward Raitt's. For she had always gone out of her way to be helpful to Agnes, and had given her holiday work in her hotel. Agnes knew she ought to be grateful, and she was.

All big Dora's luck, though, was almost cancelled out by her younger sister, Ann. Ever since her mother's death Ann Plenderleith had set out, so it seemed, to shame the Lord for having inflicted that incomprehensible loss on her. Doing good became her passion. Promoters of every charity enterprise found her zeal their greatest drawback. She press-ganged orphans from the Home into going to the manse for tea. Ruthlessly she sought out the profanest old women to take them sweets and homilies. The coming of the Americans with their Polaris submarines had given her her best opportunity to prove to the Lord that she was much bolder than He in publicly condemning what she called evil. She had taken part in every demonstration, carrying her home-made banner.

Now her family were afraid she might go religiously mad, like a great-aunt of hers sixty years ago: though Dora seemed to think it wasn't possible nowadays. Agnes could have told her that the Lord was as up-to-date as the most advanced H-bombs.

Young Ann's tragedy of course was that for her religion was not a submission to the Lord, but rather a challenge to Him: she must always be putting Him to the test. He was bound to punish her sooner or later.

Poor Dora, for all her advantages, did not count, in the Lord's eyes. Her faith in Him was too weak, too cautious, and paid too much heed to what other people thought. She was ordinary.

They were now approaching the pier. Pipe music was being played.

Agnes touched Dora's arm. "There's Ann," she said.

As she spoke she waved eagerly to the two men running to catch the ropes flung. They did not notice, and if they had would not have known she was waving to them. She had seen them at work on this pier for many years. They were old: they had grandchildren. They could not run so spryly now. They had lived useful lives, but like Ann Plenderleith, and Dora, they had never had the Lord's promise of fulfilment. Agnes had it. When ten thousand determined prayers were repaid, at compound interest, the result would be astonishing. It was going to happen soon too.

"Still like Joan of Arc," she said, laughing.

Ann's fair hair was very short and she stood straight, gazing upwards, beyond the gull on top of the mast.

"Don't be ridiculous, Agnes."

Dora had spoken sharply. She could not have said why, but Agnes knew. It was because poor Ann, so vulnerable to scoffers and lukewarm believers, was most so to her. Yet Agnes had never said anything unkind about Ann: the remark about Joan of Arc had been a compliment. Mr Tolmie, sometimes with a leather belt, had brought his daughter up to respect people socially and financially her superiors. She did it, though, with a consistency of meekness that some thought a kind of boasting.

Ann stood by the football machine, with Torch at her feet. Had he been a mastiff instead of a small fox terrier he could still have sat between them, so far apart were they: as if indeed she was about to wield a great sword.

Her navy-blue skirt was long, and her left hand was thrust into the pocket of her red blazer. She was glaring at some American sailors ready to disembark. Suddenly she came striding forward to the gangway, and stretching out her arms barred their way.

Never had she looked to Agnes more lost and pathetic. She was trying by herself to stem the advance of all the evil in the world. No wonder her little dog looked so miserable.

Then Agnes noticed him, the young American at the front, being stopped by Ann. Pale and earnest, he was the kind of lover she had often imagined. Her breasts itched. She gasped. This had happened before whenever she had seen a man she fancied, but never so violently as now. She knew the Lord had at last acted. She looked up at the sky. Never had gulls been so beautiful, so perfect, so emblematic of the Lord's power.

His hair was short and brown. His loins were slim. He was tall. Obstructed by foolish Ann, he should have pushed her aside. Instead he had taken off his cap with a courtesy fit for the presence of the Lord.

"Tickets've been taken, miss," cried a sailor behind him.

"Why should I let you pass?" cried Ann. "You are here in the service of the Devil."

"Want to feel my horns?" cried another sailor, but Agnes noticed it wasn't his brow he slyly dabbed.

His friends laughed with jolly lewdness, but Agnes's young man, still pale and earnest, laid his hand on Ann's arm. Instantly she slapped him on the face.

His mates roared with laughter. They did not seem to like him much. Agnes was pleased. He was too good for them.

An old Ardhallow woman beside Agnes was shocked.

"That shouldn't be allowed," she muttered. "I'm telling you, if she wasn't the minister's daughter, she'd be locked up."

Crying "Excuse me" Dora pushed down the gangway and dragged her sister behind a barrier of crates and milk churns.

Carrying her heavy case, Agnes made for her sailor. He needed help. He had been jostled aside by the other sailors. The little dog came creeping up to him. He stooped to pat it. It cringed back, showing its teeth.

Agnes arrived. She bumped into him deliberately. Her free hand swung against his thigh.

"Don't you know," she cried, "it's not wise to clap strange dogs?"

He turned to her with an eagerness that to her relief and delight did not instantly fade. He was not like other men. The difference was that the Lord was at work in him: he saw her as beautiful.

Only last night, on her knees in prayer, in her hostel room, she had warned the Lord that when she got home she was going to find a sweetheart, whatever her father said. For far too long she had been making love to herself. Perhaps it was why her spots had never quite cleared up.

And lo, the Lord had listened.

But He must never be embarrassed by being asked to do more than was reasonable, and He must always be given whatever help He needed. She must not expect this young man to be immediately and automatically fascinated by her: it was up to her to be fascinating.

"If you're so anxious to do a good turn," she said coquettishly, "you could carry my case out to the taxis. It's too heavy for a little girl like me."

He smiled, very politely, and at once picked up her case.

"But if you don't mind, miss," he said, "I'd like first to apologise to the young lady."

Agnes laughed, charmingly as she thought. "What young lady? Her that slapped your face? It's her who should apologise to you."

13

Just then up came Dora, almost haggard with anger. She had Ann by the sleeve.

Behind them Agnes caught sight of a small boy about twelve. Likely he was Ann's latest protégé from the Home; he was just the kind she would pick. In his eyes was a faraway look, replaced now and then by a quick suspiciousness, as if he thought he was in danger of being kidnapped. Who would ever want to kidnap him? If he had people at all they would be poor and unimportant. Paupers, Agnes had been taught, ought always to look like paupers. People had to accept their station in life, unless the Lord Himself summoned them out of it. This boy from the Home, with his refined remote face and rich-looking hair, had no business trying to look like a prince among common folk. He wasn't to be trusted.

"I don't know your name," said Dora, quite rudely.

"Dilworth, miss, Luke Dilworth."

"Well, my sister would like to apologise, Mr Dilworth."

Agnes smiled and poked him secretly in the back.

"There's no need," he said.

"Yes, there is. Go on, Ann." She lowered her voice. "If not for your own sake, then for Dad's."

Ann scowled. She glanced at Agnes, and scowled still more. "What are you smirking at?" she muttered.

"Agnes was with me on the boat," said Dora.

"I didn't strike him," said Ann.

Dora sighed in anger, Agnes sadly shook her head, and Luke lightly touched his cheek.

"I don't know him," said Ann. "Why should I strike him? I struck what he represents: evil."

He should have scorned her with a proud look. Instead he gazed at her in a dwalm of admiration. Really for a sailor he was much too simple. He had a lot to learn. Between them Agnes and the Lord would teach him.

"What nonsense, Ann," Agnes said boldly.

14

"No, no," said silly Luke. "I appreciate your stand-point, miss."

His drawl was entrancing, what he said was rubbish.

The fierceness died out of Ann's eyes: misery took its place. "If you do," she muttered, "then you must realise that these bombs you're here to look after are going to kill millions of people."

"You've got it all wrong, Ann," said Agnes, ignoring Dora's cross shake of the head.

Without knowing it perhaps Ann had done what was even worse than killing millions of people with bombs. She had called the Lord's purpose evil, whereas of course it was good, if too inscrutably so for most people to understand. Ann was like those who blamed the Lord for diseases like cancer, for children born blind or deformed, for famines in dark-skinned lands.

Luke still could not keep his eyes off Ann, in misplaced fascination.

"I would like you to know, Miss Plenderleith," he havered, "that I have attended your father's beautiful church. He is a very fine preacher."

Dora then led Ann off; between them they carried her case. The dog and the boy followed.

Luke would have preferred to carry Dora's case. Perhaps, thought Agnes, after we are married you will wish you had married someone else. I will forgive you then as I am forgiving you now.

"I know your name," she said, brightly, "so I'll tell you mine. Agnes, Agnes Tolmie. Whereabouts in America are you from?"

"North Carolina."

"Have you been in Ardhallow long?"

He was still staring ahead at Ann and Dora.

"Five weeks."

"Do you like it?"

"It's a nice little town."

"I was born here. This is me coming home from training college, for the last time, thank goodness. I'm now a certificated teacher."

"May I offer my congratulations?"

She laughed in delight. He was her young man, her new sweetheart, given to her by the Lord as Jacob had been given to Leah; and he was so courteous.

"Do you live on the ship?" she asked.

"Yes, I do."

How could they meet as lovers if he slept on the ship? Sailors made love to women on the shore, in bus shelters, in shop doorways, in people's gardens, and once even in Agnes's father's workshop; but those women were prostitutes. Agnes had her own room of course, but her father, who distrusted Americans and abominated fornicators, would take an axe to them if he were to catch them in bed.

"If you're looking for a place ashore," she said, "I can recommend one. She's a real Scots old lady."

And an old heathen who could swear better than any sailor. But her cottage was next to Agnes's.

He didn't look interested, so with a sudden inspiration she added: "That girl that slapped your face, she's been trying to reform old Granny for years."

He was instantly keen. "Miss Ann visits with this old lady?"

"Every Saturday, I believe."

Well, she thought, as they came out of the pier on to the promenade, Ann Plenderleith should feel flattered at being used to bring about what would please the Lord.

Agnes's Uncle Archie, fat as a pillar box in his bright red sweater, was standing by his taxi. Locals always slunk past; only ignorant strangers hired him. He overcharged and was surly with any that grumbled. His letters to the local newspaper, the *Ardhallow Times*, were frequent and notorious: they pointed out expensive stupidities on the part of the town council. He had himself stood as a candidate three times without success, so he had a low opinion of the intelligence of electors. He bred pedigree rabbits and had won prizes. His wife, Aunt Sadie, was always comparing him to his rabbits; and Agnes herself had noticed how, when he thought nobody was watching, he liked to let his front teeth be seen.

"Hello, Uncle Archie," she cried. "I've got you a fare. Mr Dilworth's going to the ship."

Uncle Archie rubbed his big rough nose. "Is this a click you've got, Ag? Hope no'."

But she smiled, affirming it.

"Is he the one Ann Plenderleith slapped? He looks it. God, Ag, trust you to pick one like this."

Loudly and gladly she cried, "Uncle Archie, Mr Dilworth would like you to take him first to Granny Brisbane's. He's interested in the room she's got to let."

Uncle Archie dragged the case out of Luke's grasp and heaved it into the boot. "Weel seen you've nae experience," he muttered.

"You're such a pessimist," she said, laughing. "Well, Mr Dilworth, shall we board the limousine?"

He handed her in as if she was a duchess.

Uncle Archie got into the driver's seat. "A lot mair o' a limousine than he's a stallion, if you ask me," he mumbled cryptically.

He drove away, frightening two old women on the crossing. That restored his equanimity.

"This you back a fully fledged teacher, Ag?" he asked.

"That's right," she replied, gaily.

"You'll be starting work in August?"

"That's right." In her gaiety she took Luke's arm, but immediately gave it back. Not only the Lord knew that too much too soon was to be avoided.

"But you'll be taking your usual summer job at the Arms? I was talking to her ladyship the other day. She

17

spoke very nicely about you, Ag; said you're to be sure to look her up."

"Very kind of her, I'm sure."

"You keep in wi' her, Ag. She's got the money. And Oliphant's her lawyer. You know what he is: the Convenor. You'll be looking for a job near hame. He's the man could get you one; and Miss Greenloaning's the woman could make him. I don't want to spoil your welcome back, Ag, but Sadie and me think that if your mither doesn't go into hospital soon and get that operation done then she'll not see Christmas. She's so bad that that damn brither o' mine's at last admitted his prayers have failed. Sorry, sailor, if we're boring you wi' our family troubles."

"That's all right, sir. I'm sorry, miss, your mother isn't well."

She was so pleased she took his arm again.

They were now driving along the main street. Always clean from the excessive rain, it was particularly pleasant this sunny afternoon, with flowers in the long stone troughs and tartan shields on the lamp-posts.

"Ardhallow's sure a pretty little town," said Luke.

She almost patted his hand, like a grateful bride. Born in Ardhallow, she loved it. There was Crawford the chemist's, where she had bought her first bottle of scent, which she had to apply, not behind her ears or on her bosom, but to the inside of her thighs, lest her father should smell it and call her a harlot. He *had* smelled it, but after sniffing about the house for a while had put it down to the drains which, as the cottage was over a hundred years old, were sometimes bad.

Outside McBean the greengrocer's—he was also the provost—talking to a stout woman in purple tweeds was Mr Oliphant the lawyer, dressed as usual in black. When she was a small girl Agnes had pictured the Lord as looking like this small stout self-important man; this was because she had heard him cowing her father with angry words.

"The man himself," muttered Uncle Archie.

They passed St Aidan's with its mighty steeple. The name Robert L. Plenderleith gleamed in gold letters on the board in front.

"No sign yet of the wedding," chuckled Uncle Archie. "D'you think, Ag, when she's Mrs Plenderleith the Second she'll gie awa' all her goods to feed the poor? Some think, you ken, she's capable o' it."

"I don't."

Uncle Archie turned his attention on Luke. "So you're on the lookout for a love-nest, sailor?"

Agnes laughed quietly.

"It's not that, sir," said Luke, embarrassed. "I like to read serious books. So I wish some privacy."

"What sort of books? Philosophy? Economics? Pornography?" He laughed at his own joke.

"Devotional books," said Luke, bravely.

Uncle Archie thought that was an even better joke. He laughed all the way to Agnes's cottage.

But as he was lifting her case out of the boot he became very serious. "This chap'll no' do, Ag. Where are your een? You need a young man: your Aunt Sadie and me are agreed aboot that. But no' this fellow."

Agnes's mother appeared at the door, with a dish-cloth in her hand, as if she hadn't had the energy or will either to hang it up or drop it. She looked very ill.

"Hello, Isa," called Uncle Archie. "See, I've brought Ag hame to look after you." He dropped his voice. "Have you ever tried to light a match on a bar of soap? You'd find it a damn sight easier than getting a spark of whole-some passion out of this chookie."

She did not want passion: she had none herself, so she would prefer her lover and her husband to be without it too. Passion had betrayed King David. It had slapped

Luke's face. It had made her father smash to pieces the writing desk that he had made himself and everyone had admired.

"He's a jessie-wullocks, for God's sake."

That was Ardhallow slang for an effeminate man. To be truthful, she had thought Luke a wee bit too refined for a man; but that could be praise. It did not mean, did it, that he could not make love? Standing there in the street, she tried, with her own peculiar innocence, to picture Luke naked, with his penis big and stiff, ready to make love.

"Agnes," called her mother plaintively.

"But he's a sailor, Uncle Archie."

"There's mair than one tradition aboot sailors."

She gripped him by the hand, hard. "I want you to put him down at Granny's and let him ask."

His face, with its coarse florid cheeks, big nose, and small furtive eyes, was clumsy at showing pity; and the mind behind it slow and confused.

"All right, Ag. Your faither's got a lot to answer for. Here you are, twenty-one, a trained teacher, and wi' less experience than my rabbits. Anyway, joy for you's always been different than joy for other folk."

He got into his taxi and drove the fifty yards or so to Granny's gate.

"What are you staring at?" whined Agnes's mother.

The taxi stopped. Luke got out. He hesitated, and then went through the gate. Agnes got ready to wave, but he did not look towards her.

"Take him in, Granny," she prayed.

Her mother came slowly down the path. She moaned with irritation at her pain and weakness.

"Who was that in Archie's taxi?" she asked.

"An American sailor."

"I thought so. Archie had no right to let him travel wi' you."

"I met him on the pier. He carried my case for me."

"Is he going to be staying at Granny's?"

"I don't know. I hope so."

"You hope so?" That was the old familiar shocked screech as she anticipated her husband's holy anger. Then suddenly, a new note, she spoke bitterly and flatly. "Aye, Agnes, you're right: it's time to hope. We've shivered in the shadow of your faither's prejudices too long. Time to step out into the sun that shines on other folk."

Agnes scarcely heard. Granny had come to the door. Luke had been well scrutinised. Now he was invited in.

"I could be sorry for him," went on her mother, in the same flat hostile tone, "if he'd just admit it; if he'd just say the Lord's like every other master, when you've served His turn He gets rid of you. He could have been a foreman. He could have had a business of his own. There's not a man in the country cleverer with his hands. Ask Raitt. But no, he'd to put the Lord's work first. You'll soon be independent, thank God. If you want to buy yourself scent and coloured underclothes, you can do it. He'll still call you a trollop, but you can laugh at him. What kind of a religion is it that makes you see wickedness in a doll just because it has long hair and eyes that shut?"

Suddenly the sky above Granny's cottage was bluer than it had ever been before. Gulls high in it were more than birds, they were intimations of joy. Luke had come out, looking happy. Granny was at the door. She spoke to him, he answered, both laughed.

"Archie might have had the decency to carry your case into the house," grumbled Agnes's mother.

Laughing, Agnes lifted it as if it was full of gulls' feathers.

2

"So she's still as dirty-minded as ever," said Ann, who was driving.

21

Dora had been listening to Torch in the back with the boy. He kept yelping nervously. It was Ann's fault. Like Dora and her father, poor Torch was ready to risk his life to save Ann, but did not quite know what it was she was to be saved from.

Her contemptuous remark startled Dora: for a moment she thought Elizabeth was meant.

"Agnes Tolmie," said Ann.

"Agnes?"

"Yes. And spotty."

"Ann, that's not nice. She can't help it."

"Being dirty-minded?"

"She isn't."

"Has she really taken you in? Some teacher you'll make."

Uneasily, Dora remembered what some of the girls at the college used to whisper about Agnes. She had thought they were being spiteful. It was usual nowadays to call a hypocrite anyone like Agnes who never went to dances, had never been in a theatre or cinema, read only novels prescribed for study, and every night without fail read a passage of the Bible. All the same, Agnes did have some peculiar smiles at times: it was fair to call them sly at least.

"Did you see the way she was looking at that sailor?" asked Ann.

"She was just trying to be friendly. To make up for you. For heaven's sake, Ann, what made you do it?"

"Don't change the subject. I told you why. What I detest about Agnes Tolmie and her sort is the way they get rid of responsibility on to the Lord."

"Ann, I don't want to talk about Agnes. I want to talk about you hitting that sailor. It was dreadful."

"One wee slap?"

"It could cause Dad trouble."

"And make Elizabeth sigh? She's still trying to do

away with Torch. Hints he's too old. Shivers when he goes near her. Says, so sweetly, that he smells. Is always getting his hairs on her stockings."

"She can't help it if she's got a thing about dogs."

"Just as I've got a thing about H-bombs. Is that what you mean?"

They were now driving up the drive to the Home.

"Of course not," said Dora. "And I do wish you'd try to get on better with Elizabeth. It's not fair to Dad."

They stopped at the door of the Home. There were some children who gazed with cheerful curiosity. A big girl held a small girl by the hand.

Ann got out to open the door for the boy. She put her arm round him. He suffered the embrace as Torch did Elizabeth's pats. Dora could not help smiling at the similarity.

"Listen, Tommy," said Ann. "Remember what I told you. There's nothing wrong with wanting to be by yourself."

He said nothing. Dora was struck by how thick and lustrous his brown hair was. He looked a very refined little boy. He rather reminded her of Dilworth the sailor.

When Ann released him he walked away without a word. It seemed to Dora he wasn't walking towards anything, not to the other children or to the big house. He was just walking away.

Ann got back in. The car moved off.

"Surely there *is* something wrong with wanting to be by yourself if you're only twelve or thirteen?" said Dora, looking back at the boy.

He was standing beside a tree. None of the other children went near him. Somehow her pity was spoiled by impatience with his aloofness.

"Who is he?" she asked.

"I don't know. Nobody does. He's called Tommy Springburn. That's not his real name. He was found on the doorstep of a police station in Springburn, Glasgow, inside a television box. He was just a day old. So they called him Tommy Springburn."

"Poor boy. No wonder he looks so strange." Yet, she thought, you'd have expected him to be greedy for relationships.

"He's run away from two other Homes. He's not settling in here either. Mrs Maxwell's afraid he'll take off. So he will."

"But where to, if he's got no people?"

"Not to; just away. Do you know what I think?"

Dora's heart sank. So often that arrogant question, with the voice raised, was followed by an opinion as far-fetched as it was contemptuous.

"I think he's Christ, come again to test us. We've had plenty of time to get ourselves ready."

"What nonsense. You don't think anything of the kind."

They were driving along the shore of Loch Hallow, with a view of the ugly grey hulk of the *Perseus*. A submarine lay alongside it.

"The sincerity of our faith," went on Ann, "the quality of our love: that's what's to be tested. Look at that enormous failure out there. Or are you one of those who say it really proves our love for one another? Like Elizabeth. Well, Tommy's a more intimate kind of test. Kindness isn't enough. You saw that. People sign cheques for Oxfam and Save the Children. Like Elizabeth. That's easy, too easy. All the money in the world wouldn't affect Tommy. He needs love, the kind his own mother could have given him. Which of us can do that?"

Dora laughed, in affection and annoyance. "For goodness' sake, Ann, he's just an unfortunate little boy. I'm sorry to say there must be thousands like him."

"Easy to be sorry. I'm talking about love."

Dora could not help comparing Ann's extravagance with Agnes Tolmie's quiet humility.

"What's the population of Ardhallow?" went on Ann. "About ten thousand. Surely there's among us ten true Christians? Or even five? That'd give us a pretty low mark but at least we'd pass. Where are they, though?"

Dora was about to offer their father as one, but remembered his engagement to Elizabeth. She had once overheard two women members of his congregation agreeing with each other that Miss Greenloaning with her thousands in the bank was altogether too mighty a match for a parish minister: the Lord Lieutenant of the County would be at the wedding.

Then there was his ambiguous attitude towards the Americans: he welcomed them in public, in private deplored their purpose.

"Ann," she said, trying to laugh, "you're impossible."

The manse was reached up a steep twisting drive lined with massed rhododendrons in red and purple flower. The garden was huge, with pines as high as steeples. In front of the big stone house was a lawn bordered with roses. Redder than any rose, with more glitter, was Elizabeth's Daimler. Never flamboyant in her person, she liked splendour in her cars.

Elizabeth herself, in cashmere twinset of dark blue, with a necklace of real pearls, rose out of a deck chair to greet them. People worsted by her in business thought her tranquil reasonableness false, but Dora had never heard her raise her voice in anger, not even to Torch when some of his hairs got on her stockings, nor to Ann at her most provoking.

With just the right degree of fuss she kissed Dora, embraced her, and welcomed her home. Ann she greeted cheerfully.

Dora had never seen anyone with such delicate skin as Elizabeth: on her neck especially it seemed transparent: the pearls looked heavy. Yet she never gave the impression of frailness.

Mr Plenderleith stood by, smiling, in white Fair Isle sweater. Dora saw instantly that he had heard about Ann's misbehaviour at the pier; somebody must have phoned. Though he was a big man, not yet gone to fat, and in his day on the Rugby field had dashed men heavier than himself to the ground, he always found it difficult to show authoritative anger. Perhaps his mouth was too small. Pink and handsome, he suited affability best. Not only was he anxious to think well of people, he also, if he possibly could, avoided thinking bad of them. For a man so tall he had a chirpy rather easily mocked little voice.

He too kissed Dora. He clapped Torch, too vigorously for the dog's liking. Then, with a sigh, he turned to Ann, standing feet apart, hands in her blazer pockets, an attitude Elizabeth considered unladylike.

Elizabeth indeed sighed, softly.

"Ann, my dear," he said, "I'm afraid I'm cross with you. I've just had a phone call from Mrs Crichton."

Yes, Dora had noticed that stout censorious lady on the boat. A widow, she was supposed to have said at a meeting of the Women's Guild that one marriage bed should be enough for any man of God, even if the second one had gold knobs and goose-feather pillows.

"She said, Ann," said Mr Plenderleith, attempting sternness, "that you slapped an American sailor, on the pier. Is it true?"

"She said nothing about provocation," murmured Elizabeth. "We know how provoking these sailors, some of them, can be."

"You were there, Dora," said her father. "You must have seen. What happened?"

Ann hunched her shoulders and kept contemptuously quiet.

"Well, I didn't see him provoking her," said Dora.

"Perhaps you were too far away," murmured Elizabeth. "Perhaps you didn't hear what he said."

26

"I don't think he said anything. He was very nice about it afterwards. He'll make no fuss. He said he's been to St Aidan's."

"He insulted me," said Ann, grimly. "Not in the way you think, Elizabeth. The very opposite. He tried to be friendly."

"Did he touch her at all?" whispered Elizabeth, to Dora.

"Yes, but just on the arm. Like this."

"Good grief, Ann," cried her father, "what nonsense is this?"

"He smiled at me."

"Certainly there are smiles and smiles," murmured Elizabeth.

"Are you saying, Ann," cried her father, "this was a nasty suggestive sort of smile?"

"It was a nice friendly smile."

"Ann, my dear," said Elizabeth, so quietly her pearls glittered, "you really mustn't tease us in this way."

Ann then marched right up to them, so close that all three had to retreat a little. She still advanced. Elizabeth stumbled into a rosebed.

Taller than Elizabeth, as tall as Dora, and only five inches shorter than her father, Ann glared into each of their faces in turn.

"If he'd looked at me as if he hated and distrusted me I wouldn't have hit him," she said fiercely. "If he'd looked at me in the way Elizabeth likes to imagine, as if he took me for a prostitute, I wouldn't have hit him. But he looked at me as if he took it for granted I approved of him. So I hit him. When they start using their filthy bombs," she went on, slowly and passionately, "they're not going to be able to look at me and say : But we thought you were with us, Ann Plenderleith. We smiled at you, remember, and you smiled back."

"It's not as simple as that, my dear," murmured her father with a sigh.

"For me it is." Almost in the same breath she added, "Can I use the car?"

"But Dora's just come home. We were about to have tea."

"I don't want tea. I want to go where I can think."

They knew where. At Kilcalmonell, sixteen miles away on lonely Loch Striddon, was an old forsaken kirk. Passing motorists used it as a lavatory. Ann often went there to think.

"I'd have thought you and Dora would have a lot to tell each other," said their father.

"About golf?" cried Ann, scornfully. "Well, Dad, can I?"

Though Elizabeth very slightly shook her head and he noticed it, he still nodded his own.

"Thanks. Come on, Torch." She raced for the car and bundled the dog in.

They watched her drive away. She gave them a wave such as, so Elizabeth, who had a sense of humour, said, Boadicea might have given the haughty and insolent Romans.

"Well, Dora," she went on, cheerfully, "we've got good news for you. Edgar Oliphant tells me you're to be given a post in Ardhallow school. So you'll be able to live at home."

"What about Agnes?" asked Dora. "Agnes Tolmie. Did he say what school she's being offered?"

"I'm afraid little Agnes was never in our thoughts."

"Her mother's ill. It would be better if Agnes could stay at home."

"Perhaps. Another way to look at it would be to think she'd be better removed from her father's domination. Still, she hasn't done all that well at college, has she? She can't expect the pick of the jobs. Don't you agree?"

Dora had to, though she didn't really want to. Elizabeth

was so mature and right, especially when compared with
Ann, who was so immature and wrong.

3

W HEN HE WAS only six his teacher had once said to
William Tolmie, "What is it you expect to come popping
up out of that inkwell, Willie, you're glowering it so
much?" The rest of the class had laughed, and he had
turned his glowers on them. He seldom laughed, either at
the time or in retrospect. When his joky big brother
Archie nearly got his right eye blown out keeking through
a keyhole in which a lit squib was stuck at the other end,
not a soul had thought of laughing at the time, but weeks
afterwards, when the damage was repaired, everybody
who'd seen it or who had it told to them had laughed to
tears, except wee Willie, who stayed glum.

When he had started going to the Baptist Sunday
School, on his own initiative, at the age of ten, his family
was astonished and perturbed. No Tolmie in living memory
had ever been misled by religion. His father, until he
died two years later, and thereafter his brother Archie
tried to dissuade him with entreaties, bribes, jeers,
threats, and even blows. With a scowl fit for the Devil,
Willie told them he had found God : as if it was a bloody
gold mine, Archie had said; and certainly Willie for the
next eighteen years had howked away faithfully in that
peculiar darkness, with prayers and Bible readings and
psalm dronings, until with the outbreak of war he was
called up into the Royal Engineers, for by that time he
was a journeyman carpenter.

His mother wept at his going—Archie was already in
the Argylls—but over many cups of tea she confided to
neighbours that whether Hitler was beaten or not one
blessing was that her Willie would come back from the
slaughter and the terror cured of religion.

29

. He returned with his faith refreshed by all the blood-shed, but she was dead herself by that time. He got his old job back in Raitt's. To the wonder of old Eddie, then the head of the firm, and to the annoyance of mates who worked only for wages, he put as much devotion into his work, even humdrum stuff like the framing of windows, as he did into his preaching. During his army days he had met up with a fundamentalist sect called the Church of Christ the Master, unknown in Ardhallow until he set up a branch himself. At first he was pew-maker, secretary, treasurer, proselytiser and preacher all rolled into one. In time, though, as Archie put it, he gathered round him all the gloomiest-brained bigots in the town, mercifully never more than twenty. When he got out of all that fanatical energy, Archie often muttered, God only knew.

How he came to marry so normal a lass as Isa Tennant was, according to Archie, as big a mystery as Samson's hair. Born in Ardhallow, she came of a family as healthy, in the religious sense, as the Tolmies had been before Will's infection: that was to say, she was a Protestant with too much sense to go to church. She danced, went to the pictures, liked a giggle at a blue joke, was felt more than once in the shelter in the Bishop's Glen, and at Hogmanay would drink a dram of whisky. You'd have expected her to marry a Papish priest as soon as a dreary Lordmongerer like Will Tolmie. But the wooing was short, the wedding quick, and the consummation immediately fruitful.

Jealously, for he himself was childless after five years of marriage, Archie prophesied that his brother would go on to father a tribe, like Abraham; but he was wrong. After wee Agnes was born, a tiny crab-apple of a wean, Isa's womb, like Sadie's, went barren. Once, desperate for Sadie's sake, Archie had let Will know he wouldn't mind joining him in a prayer for a son or two. Will had him on his knees for a full hour on a wooden floor, twice; so that Archie, never all that spry on his legs, was afraid he wouldn't manage to do his part even if the Lord did His. But neither painful prayer nor clumsy copulation prevailed. No other child was born to the Tolmies after Agnes.

During her prayerful infancy Agnes, a solemn wee girl, assumed that the good-natured jocularity with which her father was regarded by most people in the town sprang from respect and liking. Everybody chuckled at the sect's activities: their having to bawl their psalms like madmen when the rain stotted on their tin church; their crusades in summer on the crowded beaches; their telegrams to rebuke important people, including the Duke of Edinburgh, for desecrating the Sabbath, in his case by playing polo. To the average good-humoured Ardhallow man and woman these religious eccentricities deserved laughter more than abuse. An occasional brick, though, was tossed through the tin church's windows, pebbles and ice-cream cartons flew at the beach crusades, and letters appeared in the *Ardhallow Times* deploring their impudence in rebuking the Duke.

Agnes was only seven when she became aware of the true nature of that tolerance, though it was years later before she learned how much it mortified her father, who would so much have preferred a martyr's persecution.

He got involved in a court case. A workmate at Raitt's, a lazy slovenly man, provoked him, not with one of his obscene gibes at religion, but with the shoddiness of his handiwork. Mr Tolmie hit the botcher on the head with a piece of cheap pitch pine. As the Sheriff said it must have been wielded with great force to crack the man's skull and land him in hospital. Since there were witnesses, and Mr Tolmie dourly said he was proud he'd done it, the verdict had to be guilty, but as old Mr Raitt spoke up for him, "the maist conscientious workman I've ever employed," he was merely fined, with a warning. It was at that time that Mr Oliphant the lawyer had come to the house and shouted angrily at her father.

Afterwards the town no longer looked on her father amiably as the ringmaster of a group of bigoted clowns, good for a laugh. They were condemned as bores and hypocrites. Only if their hut turned to gold, as Archie said, would they ever be taken seriously again.

In any case the attitude of the whole of Scotland towards John Knox's style of religion had been changing. Protected by its fortress of obtuse respectability as well as by that beautiful moat, the Firth of Clyde, Ardhallow was usually slower than most places to adopt change, whether in dress or morals; but by the middle of the twentieth century leaders of local opinion like Oliphant the lawyer, 'Onion' McBean, and Falconer, Rector of the High School, had bravely recognised the need to give up certain seventeenth-century principles, mainly pertaining to the observance of the Sabbath. After much debate in the council, and in the columns of the *Times*, where Archie Tolmie had his say, the golf course, putting greens, swing parks and paddling pools were opened on Sundays. The protests of Tolmie and his like were brusquely swept aside. As Councillor McBean put it, "There used to be a time when it was Scotland's distinction to be backward in religion, but that time's long past."

As a child Agnes never putted or paddled or slid down a chute on week-days, let alone Sundays. Those children she saw perpetrating such Sabbath enormities ought, if her father was right, to suffer for it and be seen to suffer. So she waited, for hours at a stretch, for one to fall into the pond or come down the chute too fast. She was not vindictive. She did not want anyone to be hurt, but she did want her father to be proved a true prophet though despised. When at last a little boy did fall, and his face streamed blood, she was perplexed. At three was he really old enough to know what pleased the Lord and what didn't?

Her father never used endearments to her, but then

few Scots fathers did, after their daughters were over the age of seven or eight. What he did do that was unusual if not unique was to address her "as if she was Job's granny", which was how her mother put it. "She's just a wee lassie, Will. Mind that." But he had not minded it, and had continued to use an Old Testament gravity and severity on his small daughter.

They sometimes went walks together, along the esplanade or up the Bishop's Glen. Gradually it dawned on her that she wasn't company for him. No one was. When she had whispered this discovery to her mother the latter retorted, "Hasn't he got the Lord?" Agnes was reassured for a while, until she began to suspect that he didn't even have the Lord, that he could not see himself as one of the chosen.

One frosty night, a few days before Christmas, Agnes was finishing off a pair of bedsocks she was knitting for Granny Brisbane. Suddenly from the shed in the garden where her father was putting finishing touches to a writing desk she heard a great yell of despair and then a crashing and splintering. Ignoring her mother's cry from upstairs to "leave him alone, he could be dangerous", she rushed down the slippery path to the shed. Boldly she opened the door.

The first thing she saw was the writing desk, smashed. If wood had blood she saw and smelled it then. This writing desk, in inlaid mahogany, had seemed to her his masterpiece. It had refreshed her love for her lonely, taciturn, gloomy, glowering father to see, in this beautiful piece of workmanship, a happiness and fulfilment that he was never able to show in his relationship with her or her mother.

Now it was ruined. It was as if he had killed himself. The axe was still in his hand. He was in tears.

Long since convinced of her own election by the Lord she understood and sympathised with her father in his

33

terrible disappointment. He had himself taught her that the Lord's will, though always incalculable and often hard to endure, must still be endured. She prayed for him, earnestly, but not too insistently. His own prayers, so much longer and more numerous, had been hearkened to and denied; hers, if too urgent, would be impertinent. One thing her father had induced in her was a feeling for what the Lord would stand, and what He wouldn't.

In school, while parsing or drawing maps or working out algebra equations, she'd shiver with delight as her soul tasted the sweetness of knowing the Lord favoured her. That the marks of His favour were still to be shown made them all the sweeter. Her classmates, as they glanced at her, winked to one another and touched their heads with their forefingers, meaning that she was daft. All they could see in her were irrelevant trivial inferiorities like her smallness, her not being pretty, her skirts being the longest in the school, her being forbidden to go to the cinema or to read comics. They did not know yet she had a superiority over them too great to be named. The time would come, though, when they would see for themselves.

4

IT WAS HER father who brought in the news that Luke Dilworth had moved into Granny Brisbane's. At the tea table he remarked surlily that there seemed to be a young man staying next door.

"An American from the look of him. No shame. Outside in broad daylight hanging up clothes. I wouldn't be surprised if he'd washed them himself."

"If he did, Will Tolmie," said his wife, for whom he'd never washed as much as a teaspoon, "isn't it to his credit he should be willing to oblige an old woman over eighty and tortured with pain?"

"If she's in pain, Isa, who has she to thank for it?"

He meant that Granny was a notorious sinner: she had earned her punishment of aching joints. In that very cottage next door she had slept with a soldier on leave while her own man was away fighting in France, in the 1914 war. She had had a baby to her lover. It had died within a week, and her lover had gone back to the battle-field to be killed. Mr Tolmie had been only eight at the time, yet he maintained he could remember the adulterer, John McKenzie, a curly-haired man in a kilt, always laughing and always ready with a penny for any child that looked sad. Mr Tolmie granted him that human kindness, and yet had said many times he was glad he was now repenting in hell.

Agnes was sure her father was thinking then of John McKenzie. As he prepared to say grace, he added, more tolerantly: "I just don't think it's manly for a young man to be seen hanging out such clothes."

Then he began his long grumble of thanks, while his daughter wondered not about the munificence of the Lord Who had provided their fried eggs and sliced sausage, but about what sort of clothes Luke had hung out.

Grace over, Agnes jumped up and went into the kitchen to take the food out of the oven. Her father often grumbled that the food not being on the table in front of them spoiled the grace, but her mother always retorted that she wasn't going to eat stone-cold sausages for anyone. If they grued at what was on their plates, wasn't that an even worse mockery of the grace?

From the kitchen window no view could be had of Granny's drying-green, but Agnes was well practised in opening the back door quietly. Only three skips took her to a spot where, by a number of leaps, she could make out the items of Granny's washing. Luke himself wasn't there, but two of his shirts were, white, shining in the sun, a towel, and a pair of Granny's long flannel drawers. For a moment Agnes imagined him wearing one of those shirts

35

and nothing else. Uncle Archie was wrong. Luke was as virile as any man. She could see he was.

Back in the living-room she found her mother trying to get her father to admit that if Granny's pains were punishment for past sins, so was his own sore back which he had been complaining about for months. Not to mention her own pains and chronic tiredness.

"Very likely, Isa," he said, mildly.

Agnes pitied them both. They had no joy like hers. The moment the dishes were washed she would slip over to Granny's.

"Have you been to see Miss Greenloaning about that job, Agnes?" asked her father.

His wife pounced again. "So you're in a hurry to see your only daughter spending her hard-earned holidays washing thousands of dishes, while Dora Plenderleith—though I've nothing against Dora who's always been friendly to me and helpful to Agnes—while she, and lots of others not half as deserving as Agnes, go about in motor cars and swim in the sea and play golf. Even on Sundays."

He always found it hard to condemn people the Lord had placed above him. It was the sort of simpleness that made him vulnerable.

"Anyway," said Agnes, "I was thinking of trying elsewhere this year. There are lots of hotels wanting girls. Why should I go to her?"

"Because she's been good to you," said her father, "and she pays the best wages."

"So money's everything, is it?" jeered his wife.

The gibe was bitter not because he thought too much of money but because he had always thought too little of it. Thus he had kept himself and his family poor. His fine pieces of furniture, for which he could have got fifty pounds and more, he had given away for nothing, as presents. In Oliphant's big yellow house there was a sideboard her Will had made. Oliphant had at first declined the gift, but when he had seen it he'd quickly changed his mind: his offer to pay for it had been refused. Other influential men in the town, worthy ex-provosts, with motto'd lamp-posts outside their gates, had received similar gifts. Their houses, Will had said, with large rooms and high ceilings, would show off his pieces better than his own small cottage. When she'd pointed out to him that he could sell them, to Barbour, the Ardhallow dealer in high-class furniture, or to a Glasgow firm, he had said he did not wish to dishonour the talent the Lord had given him. "You take wages from Raitt, don't you?" she had cried, thinking he was being stupid again. But Agnes had understood and respected him. Following his example, she had become used to having few possessions.

"Agnes," he said, not looking at her, "I want you to stay away from Granny's, in the meantime."

"No. Why should she?" cried her mother. "Granny's our friend. Why should she stop visiting her?"

"You know why, woman."

"Will Tolmie, you've got a filthy mind, that's why. This is a decent boy. Otherwise Granny would never have taken him in."

"What kind of judge is she?"

"I shouldn't be surprised you hold something against her that happened nearly fifty years ago. Forgiveness was never in your nature."

He looked at her with a peculiar appeal in his eyes. Somehow he reminded Agnes of a dog confronted by a situation it couldn't understand.

"Why are you always finding fault with everything I say, Isa?" he asked.

"Because I'm dying, that's why; and you'll not let me go into hospital. Oh no, you'll pray and I'll get better. I've been ill for years, Will. Likely what's wrang wi' me's gone too far for cure. Didn't Dr Armstrong say as much."

"You know I've given permission for the operation. It's yourself that's against it."

Agnes knew why. A similar one had been performed on a neighbour a few months ago and she had promptly died. People whispered that if she had been left alone she would still have been alive.

An hour later, when her father was lying down on his bed to ease his back, Agnes got ready to go over to Granny's and see Luke. Her mother helped. She put on a blue-and-white dress that Dora Plenderleith had once admired; it wasn't quite as long as her others. She dabbed scent behind her ears; she even applied a little lipstick.

"I don't like you disobeying your father, Agnes," whimpered her mother, "but he's got to realise you're over twenty-one and entitled to your own life. You deserve happiness. God knows you've had little of it up to now. You've been patient."

"My time's coming, Mum."

"Aye, but don't throw yourself at this boy. Get to know him first. Be careful. You've had no experience. Bring him to see me. We can arrange it when your father's down at his kirk."

"Who's racing on ahead now, Mum?"

"Well, I'll admit I'd like to see you settled wi' some young man that'll be kind to you, before I dee."

"You're not going to die for ages yet."

"I'd like to hold a grandwean in my arms."

Agnes laughed. "I'll do my best."

"You said his name was Luke? That ought to please your faither; it's a Bible name. Mind, don't stay too long."

Again Agnes laughed, gaily. "It depends."

Tiptoeing past her father's room, she heard him groaning. If his back was as sore as that, or his soul as disturbed, then it wasn't likely he'd get up to spy on her out of the window.

All the same she was as cautious as Mick, Granny's cat, as she squeezed through the hedge between the two gardens, crept through the long grass and nettles, and arrived at the drying-green. She could not resist touching one of the shirts.

She banged loudly on the back door before she opened it. "One big bang, Agnes," Granny had demanded. "For a' you ken, I micht be in bed wi' big Plenderleith the minister."

She shouted from the living-room: "Wha's that? Is it you, Agnes?"

"Yes, it's me."

As Agnes passed through the kitchen she looked for signs of Luke. On a shelf was a tin of coffee. Granny always drank tea. It must be Luke's. She went over, picked it up, and kissed it lightly.

Out in the passage she paused at the door of the room that would be Luke's. Granny's house was all on the one level. She listened for sounds of him, but heard none. He must be in the living-room with Granny.

"Whit's keeping you?" cried Granny. She sounded sleepy.

"I'm coming, I'm coming." She went eagerly.

But he wasn't in the living-room. Granny was alone, happed up in a tartan shawl in her creaky old rocking-chair. Her hair was whiter than Agnes had ever seen it before. In both hands she held the pewter mug that her long-dead husband had won at bowls: it had scenes from Tam o' Shanter depicted on it. In it now, from the smell, and from Granny's mischievous lip-smackings, was beer. An empty bottle stood on the table, on top of the red-and-white checked cloth; another lay on its side under her chair, sniffed at by old Mick.

"So it's you, Miss Tolmie," she cried, with her haughtiest cackle. "Time for a change of toast. Brisbane there never appreciates it." This was her husband, in a faded photograph on the chiffonier: he wore a high stiff collar and a lugubrious smile. "So, Agnes, here's to you." She took a sly sip. "And here's to your mither." Another sip. "And here's to your faither." Another sip. "And here's to the Lord." This time she held the mug at her mouth until she'd emptied it.

"I'd have thought," said Agnes, laughing, "that you'd have drunk to your new lodger, seeing it was probably him that brought you the beer."

"Aye, it was, and don't you go blaming him for it. He drinks orange juice himself. Agnes, I've found a treasure. If he was my ain grandson he couldn't be kinder."

She never had any grandchildren. Her nickname was a mystery.

"You didn't exactly find him, Granny. I gave him to you."

"You're in a sciegh mood. Come here. That's a braw dress. Hae you got lipstick on? D'you smell something, Mick? Agnes, you besom, you're scented."

"Where is he?"

"So that's it? He's the fish that's brought you sniffing. Well, Aggie, you could do a lot worse. He'd suit you fine. He's damn near as holy as your faither, but it maks him kind and happy, as it should. He's made me change my mind aboot Yanks."

"Well, where is he?"

"Gone to play gowf. Young Raitt and the elder Plenderleith lassie came for him in their caur."

For a few moments Agnes felt panicky, as if something of great value had been stolen from her. After the golf they would go back to the manse for supper. He would meet Ann there.

Well, there was no danger in that. Ann would either snub him or slap his face again.

"So the Plenderleiths are showing an interest in him?" she asked.

40

"It's because that daft faggot Miss Ann slapped his face. They're trying to make up for it. Not that he's got any grudge against her. He's got a grudge against naebody, that boy. He's good. Different from you, Agnes."

"Why, am I not good, Granny?"

"Aye, but you juist do it to please the Lord."

"Isn't that why everybody's good?"

"Luke does it because it's his nature. I could see you up to mischief if it suited you, Agnes. But not Luke. He'll be taken advantage of, sorry to say. Luke got me to wash my hair. Sorted my wireless set. Scrubbed the kitchen floor. Bought me this beer. Is going to hire a television, and to mend my gate that's been broken a year, and your faither that's a man o' God has walked past it a thoosand times, a joiner to trade, and never once offered to fix it. Tell you whit though, lass. Talking's made me thirsty again; forby, it's warm in here. So though I promised myself to drink juist the one bottle I think I'll hae anither. Fetch it, that's a good girl. They're in a box under the sink."

"There's another empty bottle under your chair, Granny."

"Aye, that was Mick's. Go on, Agnes. Nae need for the Lord to ken."

"All right, as long as Luke doesn't blame me for getting you drunk."

When she came back with the bottle she found that Granny had dozed off, clutching the tankard. She was snoring. Mick was purring. Mr Brisbane in the photograph looked sadder than ever. The two china dogs on the chiffonier beside him glittered, ready to bark.

Agnes stole along to Luke's room, her heart beating fast. She knew it well: she had once slept in it herself for over a month when her own house was being altered. This was the same hard bed, covered with the same faded pink quilt. When she had turned it had squeaked, as if a dozen

41

mice were beneath. Gasping, with one hand clutching her breasts and the other her crotch, she imagined herself and Luke in that bed making love. She felt joyful and excited. The Lord in His benevolence had given men and women organs that fitted each other so well, and responded to each other like flowers that rose or opened with the sun. Surely He would have put pain there instead of unimaginable pleasure if He had looked on the sliding of the man's big hard proud thing into the woman's soft meek open slippery thing as filthy. Her father was very wrong. Perhaps it was the reason why he had been rejected.

She felt so weak and dizzy with that joy and excitement that she had to sit down on the edge of the bed, her legs trembling.

She looked round the room. No one else would have thought it beautiful. The wardrobe door still did not shut properly. The window snib was still broken. "Wha do you think's going to crawl in and steal you, Agnes?" On the dressing-table mirror were two yellowish blemishes. "My een, spying on you, Agnes." The waxcloth was worn with age: it once had been red roses. The only carpet was a strip with a hole in it beside the bed.

She went over to the wardrobe. Luke's clothes were in it. She took out a pair of lilac-coloured slacks and pressed them against her face; she sniffed at them greedily. Her legs felt weak again. "I must love him," she thought. "I wouldn't feel like this if I didn't." And indeed she felt she knew him and loved him better than she did anyone else, including her father and mother.

On the dressing-table was a coloured photograph about the size of a postcard. It showed a man and a woman and two girls seated on the porch of a shabby-looking house. They were all very ordinary. The elder of the girls had curlers in her hair; the younger was giggling. Elizabeth Greenloaning would think them scruff; so would the Plenderleiths. The more Agnes gazed at them the more she liked them: their ordinariness put Luke within her reach. They were his parents and sisters. After all, Agnes was a trained teacher. These girls, well, the younger might be still at school, the other probably worked in a shop or factory. They weren't pretty. Their names, as she discovered when she looked at the back, were Cheri and Yvonne. Elizabeth Greenloaning would think such names for such people ridiculous, though she would be too well-mannered to say so. Agnes thought they were lovely names, such as Luke's sisters should have.

Also on the dressing-table, handy for reading in bed, was a Bible. Luke's name was written on it in a very fancy handwriting, with long loops and flourishes. Somehow she was sure it was Luke's own writing. It didn't mean he was effeminate: it just meant that when he was a small boy at school learning to write his teacher had insisted on this kind of lettering.

Her legs grew weak again as she imagined that earnest small boy.

On the low mantelpiece was a row of books. Their titles impressed her but worried her too: *Christian Ethics*; *Being a Christian in a Difficult World*; *Temptations Withstood*; and *In Hand with God*. Taking one's Christianity seriously was worth great praise, and she could never have loved a cynical believer like Edward Raitt; but there was always the danger that, unless you had acquired Agnes's way of looking at things, you might think making love nasty, only to be condoned between married couples, and even then with reluctance. That was her father's attitude. She prayed that it wasn't Luke's.

There was one title that worried her for a different reason: *Christians and the Bomb*. Glancing through it she gathered it argued the viewpoint that genuine Christians could never approve of weapons of mass destruction. Perhaps Ann Plenderleith had lent it to him. That slap on the face had not satisfied her. She was determined to disgrace and ruin him.

Granny was calling, peevishly.

She hurried back to the living-room.

Granny had managed to open the bottle and had it at her mouth like a baby.

"Whaur hae you been?" she mumbled, suspiciously.

"In the kitchen, tidying up."

"Whit was there to tidy? He did it before he went oot. You've been up to something, Agnes. I can tell."

Agnes laughed. "What could I have been up to?"

"In your heid, I mean. You and the Lord." She took a long drink. "Weel, we'll see."

"What will we see, Granny?"

"Never you mind. It's time you found a young fellow, one that wouldn't tak advantage o' you. We'll see."

"That's right, Granny, we'll see. Is there anything you'd like me to do for you before I go? I told my mother I wouldn't be long."

"You can put these bottles in the waste-bin. How is your mither?"

"She's talking about going into hospital."

"Let's hope she does and it's a success."

"I'll be going then."

"Juist a minute. Come here."

Agnes went over. The old woman seized her hand and stared up into her eyes for almost half a minute, during which Agnes heard Mick purr, Granny wheeze, the clock tick, and her heart sing.

"We'll see," said Granny, and let go.

What she was saying was that she would help Agnes to obtain Luke as a sweetheart.

"But tak it easy, Agnes. You've been patient a long time. Be patient a bit longer."

"Yes, Granny."

Before going home she stood under Granny's hawthorn

tree that was thick and sweet with flourish, for ten minutes, and thought about Luke.

5

AGNES WAS PREPARED to take it easy, but not too easy. Leah hadn't got Jacob as her husband just by sitting in her tent and waiting for him to come and claim her. Prompted by the Lord, she'd sneaked in the dark into Jacob's tent and on to his bed; pretending to be her sister Rachel she'd got him to make love to her. Whether it was very painful, as it could be for a virgin, or very pleasurable, she had been intelligent and brave enough to utter no groan of pain or whimper of joy. Therefore her pretence was not discovered until too late, when Jacob's seed was in her, the most solemn and indissoluble of promises. He had had to fulfil her week and marry her. Of all the women in the Bible, Leah was Agnes's favourite.

As determined as Leah, though hardly with her father's connivance, she lay in wait for Luke at every safe opportunity. On week-days he was at work on board the *Perseus* from eight till five. She was able to catch a bleary fond glimpse of him leaving Granny's shortly after seven. Her own father was having breakfast then. At half past five when Luke returned it was awkward, for her father came home at the same time. After tea her father watched her like a jailer. Even if he lay down to rest his back he kept shouting down and she had to answer.

It was almost a week before she got a chance to speak to Luke. Even then it was the briefest of conversations. She met him on Granny's path. He was about to pass her with a pleasant smile and "good evening", but she stepped in front of him.

"Remember me?" she asked, coyly.

"Sure. How are you, Miss Tolmie?"

45

"Agnes, please. We're neighbours, aren't we? I'm going to call you Luke."

"I sure would like that, Agnes. But you'll have to excuse me. I'm already late for an appointment."

He slipped past and was off before she could grab him by the fawn jacket or lilac-coloured slacks. Not that she tried to, of course. But as she gazed after him she whispered, "Who is your appointment with, Luke Dilworth? It should be with me."

When she went in she found Granny wouldn't talk to her: she was too interested in the television.

"It's a lot of damned nonsense," muttered the old woman, but she waved Agnes to be quiet when she asked if Granny knew whom Luke had gone to meet.

Next day, and the next, and the next, when she called after tea, scented, lipsticked, and wearing one of her new bras that showed off her breasts, he quickly rose from his stool in the living-room and went into his own room.

Granny was still new-fangled with the television. "Don't be in too big a hurry," was all she would say, in an off-hand manner.

Agnes waited for the week-end; or rather for Saturday afternoon: Sunday was given up to the Lord, with three services in the tin church, and the rest of the day spent under her father's gloomy surveillance.

But when she arrived at Granny's, about three o'clock, she found Luke had gone off to visit Inverary Castle.

"Who with?"

"The twa Plenderleith lasses, and a boy frae the Home."

"Ann too?"

"She was driving. She brought me these." Granny pointed to a poke of black-striped balls lying on the table. "She's improved. She seems to hae come to her senses."

"I know what she's up to."

"And whit's that?"

"She's trying to get Luke to desert or something. What

46

a triumph that would be for her. He'd be disgraced. How she'd laugh."

"Agnes, you're a bad wee tinker putting sich thoughts in the lass's heid."

"Then why's she pretending to be friendly with him? You know she hates everybody connected with the Bomb."

"Luke's an awfu' easy boy to be freen's wi'. Naebody could hate him."

"His mates do."

"How do you ken that, Agnes?"

"Because he's better than them, that's why."

"Well, keep calm. It's no' like you to get a' worked up. Whaur's your famous patience?"

"Why is she friendly with him?"

"Because she likes him, I wad say."

"Likes him?"

"Aye, but no' in the way you're thinking. Her mind's still on higher things. No' like ours, Agnes eh?"

"I'm serious, Granny. Whatever her intentions, she's bound to have a bad influence on him."

"I don't see that. She's tried her damnedest to get me to gie up beer, swearing, farting, and lifting up my skirts to warm my dainty at the fire. You could hardly ca' that being a bad influence. Listen, Agnes, you doit, I ken fine whit's bothering you: you're jealous. Whaur's your patience? You used to be an example to us a'. Disappointed in this, in that, in damn near everything, you used to say it didnae matter, your turn wad come, you had the Lord's word for it."

"So I have."

"Well then, wait."

"I'll wait."

But after she had waited for another three weeks, with Luke politer than ever and more evasive, Granny took her by the hand.

47

"I'm sorry, Agnes," she said. "It's no' going to work."

"Yes, it is."

"Turn that bluidy thing off. You cannae hear yourself think these days."

Agnes turned the television off.

"Whit folk get paid for! He's no' interested, Agnes. You micht as weel face it."

"He is, Granny, really."

"Then why does he no' show it?"

"He's shy."

"He is, but I doot if that's the reason."

"He's afraid of my father."

"That maks sense."

"My father stopped him in the street and warned him to keep away from me."

"The clown of a man. Didn't he ken he was trampling on your gairden o' flowers? Does he ken you're sweet on this boy?"

"I don't know. Mum does."

"Then your faither's bound to. Your mither tortures him wi' hints. She wouldn't keep quiet aboot this. Anyway, lass, the very birds in the gairden ken it; so does Mick; so do the worms in the ground, the way your feet hae been dancing. Whit saddens me is that young Luke's just the boy for you. Does your faither no' realise they're damn scarce, the kind that wad suit you? I don't mean onything unkind by that, lass; it's juist that you've had sich a bluidy ridiculous upbringing. Your faither should be doon on his knees thanking the Lord for sending Luke your way, instead o' sharpening his axe."

"He doesn't like Americans."

"Because of that one he found spurtling the wee whure in his shed?"

"He didn't like them before that."

"It cannae be because o' their bombs. Your faither wad like nothing better than to see us a' blown up."

48

"Granny, I've still got hope."

Granny sighed. "Agnes, he's looked and then he's looked awa'. No' even the Lord can mak him look again. And I've put in a good word for you whenever I could. Try elsewhere, Agnes. Join anither church. Whit aboot Greenloaning's hotel where you wash the dishes? Aren't there any young sparks hanging aboot it that you could try for?"

"He'll come to me, Granny, I know it."

"Presented by the Lord, is that it?"

"Yes, Granny, that's it."

"Agnes, you're too auld now for sich beliefs. I mind the day when you came crawling across my doorstep wi' something clutched in your wee fist; you were only three at the time. It was a big black clock, a beetle that is. 'Whaur'd ye get that horrid thing?' says I. 'The Lord gie'd it to me,' says you. You believed it then, Agnes, you cannae believe it noo."

"Why not, Granny? Everything comes from the Lord."

"Even disappointments. And you've had your share."

"I'm not going to be disappointed, Granny. Luke's mine. You'll see."

"Aye, lass, I'll see."

From her sigh it was evident that what Granny expected to see was Agnes disappointed again. Before it had been the doll with long hair, the bicycle, and the fiddle; now it would be Luke. But Agnes with an effort had been able to appreciate her father's reasons for denying her those other things. Not even he would ever convince her that to possess Luke would corrupt her soul. The truth was, not to possess him would.

6

ONE SATURDAY, AGNES, still alert, heard a car stopping at Granny's gate. She hurried out. It was the Plenderleiths', driven by Ann, wearing a white dress. The door opened and down jumped the little white dog; he began to bark, in fun, at old Mick asleep in the branches of the hawthorn tree, whose blossom was now withered.

The horn sounded. Luke came running out of Granny's house. He wore his lilac-coloured slacks and a pink shirt. The sun gleamed on his hair. He looked very happy.

"Wait," cried Agnes, and pulling open her gate she ran along the street towards them.

The dog came scampering to greet her. Its friendliness was in contrast to Luke's quick, ashamed but stubborn turning away. Ann stared out, amused. The orphan boy in the back showed not so much a lack of interest as neutrality; Agnes was to remember this later.

"You're in a great hurry," said Ann, laughing, "with your apron on."

"Where are you going?" gasped Agnes.

"Up the glen, to show Luke the old castle."

"The ruins? Can I come? I did a project on it at college."

"We're just going to look at it, not write a historical account."

"Still, it's more interesting to know something of the history. They say," she added, turning to Luke, "Robert the Bruce stayed in it six hundred years ago."

"And Mary Queen of Scots too, no doubt," said Ann, sarcastically.

"So she did, Ann."

"Is there an old castle in Scotland she didn't stay at? But you can come if you like. I don't mind. Neither does Torch. What about you, Tommy?"

The boy showed he understood by smiling ever so faintly.

"What about you, Luke?" asked Ann. "Are you applying your veto?"

Agnes smiled at him with all the appeal she could. He did not immediately nod or say she was welcome. Only a few seconds of hesitation, but it was enough to stun Agnes and raise Ann's brows.

Watching through the curtains Granny shook her head.

"I don't mind," he said.

In a moment Agnes had her apron off. Afraid that if she took it into Granny's they would drive off without her, she hung it up on the hawthorn near Mick. Then she got into the car at the back beside the boy. She was glad she had her red skirt and her rather tight jumper. Her breasts might not be better than Ann's but they were more noticeable.

"We'll leave the car at Sodger's Brig," said Ann. "It's called that," she explained to Luke sitting beside her, "because a soldier on leave from the 1914 war killed himself by jumping from it. They say he was depressed because he had to go back to the trenches where he'd seen so much slaughter."

"I heard it was because his sweetheart had jilted him," said Agnes.

"Very likely he was just drunk," said Ann. "But if Agnes wants it to be a romantic tragedy don't let's spoil it for her."

She laughed, not very maliciously. She seemed relaxed, as if Luke's presence was good for her. But Agnes, watching with almost frantic closeness, saw that Granny was right, Ann was not in love with him. Far worse, though, he was with her. Or rather he worshipped her. He gazed at her all the time. Whatever she said, and most of it was nonsense, he listened with a delight he couldn't contain. He tried to disguise it with excessive politeness, but Agnes wasn't deceived.

The dog licked her hand. She let it for its pink tongue going in and out reminded her, quite unobscenely, of the love-making she had dreamt of between her and Luke, and which would never take place if she or the Lord did not do something soon.

51

She could think of nothing.

They got out of the car at the bridge. Leaning over the mossy parapet, through the screen of beech leaves, they gazed down at the rocks in the burn where the soldier's body had been shattered. Two wagtails hopped off and on them now.

"Well, it's better to be alive," remarked Ann, as she led the way along the path past the sign forbidding rubbish to be dumped. Luke hurried to walk beside her. His very buttocks in the lilac-coloured slacks were in thrall to Ann, but even so Agnes burned to go down on her knees and fondle and kiss them. She would save him from Ann.

Meanwhile she would walk with the boy and wait for the Lord's intervention. This must come. Her faith was too valuable for the Lord to lose.

She had heard from Granny that the boy had been found on the doorstep of a police-station, and therefore had no people. "Tells you nothing," Granny had grumbled. "Mick's a blether by comparison."

"What's your name?" asked Agnes.

"Tommy."

"Not just Tommy surely."

"Tommy Springburn."

Who said he wouldn't talk to anyone? He was even smiling.

"How old are you, Tommy?"

"Twelve."

"So you'll be going to the High School after the holidays?"

"Yes."

"Do you like school?"

This time he was silent. Tactfully, she did not ask again. Many children did not like school: it did not mean they were bad or weak-minded or unsociable. She had not liked school herself. When she was a teacher the children in her class, she vowed, would love it.

The wagtails seemed to be following them, flitting from one clump of ferns to another. Other birds sang. High up in the sky, far above the tallest tree, gulls soared. The Lord was watching. She need have no fear.

Ann and Luke were well ahead. She turned once to see where they were, but he didn't: he deliberately kept looking the other way.

"Do you like staying at the Home?" asked Agnes.

"No," after a long pause.

"I'm sure they must treat you all right."

He shrugged his shoulders.

"Who are your friends?"

He said nothing.

"You must have some special friends. Tell me about them."

But why must he? She had had none when she was his age. She had none now.

She studied him, and again was struck by the curious richness of his hair, and the extraordinary thoughtfulness of his face. At his age she, without friends, had had thin dull hair. But had she, with her many prayers, looked as thoughtful as this? They had all laughed at her, winking and prodding their brows with their fingers. They had not understood why she had looked so much more dedicated than they. They believed only in themselves, therefore they believed in nothing. Perhaps this boy who had no friends and could not settle at school or at the Home, among people that was to say, was too close to the Lord and so must, like her, look different and be despised for it.

"Do you go to Sunday school?" she asked.

He nodded. She remembered that as a Home orphan he would be obliged to go. She had seen them in procession: their attendants, in kind but uncommitted voices, had told them to keep in line and not talk so much. It was the same in day schools: there the children were ordered to attend the morning assemblies, recite the Lord's Prayer, sing a hymn, and listen to the Bible-reading. There was nothing wrong with that: left to themselves children would become pagans. What was wrong, as she had pointed out to Mr Falconer himself, the Rector, and to several of the teachers, was that those who demanded that the children honour the Lord did not in their hearts honour Him themselves.

Suddenly, ahead, were loud angry voices and coarse laughter. The dog barked frantically.

Agnes ran forward. In a plantation on the hillside close to the path three boys, fourteen or so years of age, were uprooting a young tree about the height of a yacht mast; it shook as if in a storm. Other trees had already been torn up. The vandals were enjoying their evil, especially as Ann Plenderleith was screaming to them to stop. They made obscene gestures to her: they enjoyed these too.

Ann turned to Luke, as if expecting him to leap to the rescue. He stood as still as a tree. He was very pale. He seemed to be rigid with fear.

"Well," thought Agnes, as she arrived panting beside him, "I don't care if you're a hero or not."

As he turned to her he smiled. A stranger might have thought he was in love with her. It was because she had seen the nakedness of his cowardice. He was in her power.

One of the boys was as big as and stronger than Luke; the other two were tough and violent. They were from Glasgow. They could have knives. Two had heavy sticks, one an iron bar.

The little dog thought they were playing. It decided to join in. Ignoring Ann's cry, it dashed at them with growls of pretended ferocity. The one with the iron bar, startled, swiped out. It thudded against the dog's head. Blood appeared like magic. With dwindling yaps of pain and astonishment the dog crumpled to the ground.

With a scream Ann scrambled up the bank to her dog.

Its murderers snarled at her, like animals. They brandished their weapons. One, the biggest, who looked half-witted, stuck his stick between his legs so that it protruded like a gigantic penis. He advanced on Ann as if to rape her with it.

Clutching her dog, she screamed and screamed. She frightened them. "Fuck you," they yelled, and fled up through bracken and foxgloves. They paused to glare back. Ann still screamed. "We never touched you, big fucking fool. Mind your own fucking business next time."

"We'd better help her," said Agnes.

Kneeling, Ann held the dog tight. Her dress was red with blood, as if she was menstruating. The way she kept bending forward her knickers could be seen; only they weren't knickers but briefs; they were white too.

Luke from below must see them and her big thighs. He must also see that, confronted by actual evil for the first time in her life, she had lost her nerve completely. Agnes, on the other hand, had remained cool and undismayed.

In the distance now the boys were yodelling obscenely and blasphemously.

The dog was certainly dead; its eyes were glazed. It seemed to be whimpering, with sudden yells; but this was Ann. She looked almost as insane as she sounded.

"Ann," urged Agnes, "let it go. It's dead. Let me take it from you. Look at your dress."

Ann would not let go. Her faith in herself was gone: that was why she was holding on so tightly to her dead dog.

Luke came forward. A middle-aged couple were approaching along the path.

"I'm sorry," he mumbled. "I should have—"

"She doesn't hear you," said Agnes. "What could you have done? They were three to one. They're not Ardhallow boys; they're from Glasgow. Perhaps they had knives. Anyway, as an American you did best to keep out of it."

"D'you think so, Agnes?" he mumbled.

"Of course."

He looked at her with a gratitude that could easily be turned into love. The Lord had intervened: He had arranged for those boys to despoil the trees, kill the dog, humiliate Luke, derange Ann, and give Agnes her chance.

Ann became aware of them. She stared at Luke in revulsion. "It's your fault," she whimpered.

He thought she meant that if he hadn't been a coward her dog wouldn't have been killed. Perhaps she did, but Agnes wondered if she was, with insane cunning, insinuating that, since he was associated with the Bomb, in her view the source of all evil and violence, then the iron bar had in a sense been wielded by him.

"Listen, Ann," said Agnes. "There are people coming. Get control of yourself. Don't exaggerate. Three young brutes have killed your dog—to be fair it was half an accident—and insulted you. That's awful, but it's nothing unusual, things like that happen every day, not in Ardhallow perhaps but in other places, they've been happening for thousands of years, and they'll go on happening, perhaps for ever. We don't let them defeat us, that's all."

The man and woman arrived. They knew who Ann was. They were shocked and solicitous. They said the boys should be birched.

Agnes thought the dog should be buried there among the trees, but Ann, though she did not say it, was determined to take it home. Perhaps, Luke whispered, she wanted to bury it in the manse garden. He suggested it humbly.

They set off down the path to the car. Luke would drive them to the manse. Agnes and he kept close to Ann to screen her from the affronted stares of people out for a quiet afternoon stroll.

They were not far from the car when they came upon Tommy seated on a bench by the side of the path. He could not have looked more unconcerned if he had been licking an ice-cream cone.

Ann saw him. She seemed to be seeing nothing else, her eyes were as glazed as the dog's; but she noticed Tommy at once. Like a woman her dead child, she showed him the dog, piteously. He glanced at it with little more interest than when it was alive.

"Why did they do it, Tommy?" she whispered.

"He's just a child, Ann," said Agnes. "How can he tell you?"

But Tommy answered. "For fun."

"Fun?" Ann shrank back in horror.

"It was fun to them," said Agnes. "He's right. Isn't every evil thing that's done fun to the person that does it? You needn't worry, though. They'll be punished, if not now, if not in this world, then in the next. They'll not escape. They'll laugh on the other side of their faces."

7

THEY DROVE STRAIGHT to the manse. Agnes sat in front with Luke. Now and then she squeezed his arm: it was to reassure him that as he was now hers she would tell no one about his timidity, and also that, with her to look after him, he wouldn't need to be brave.

She was so happy she had difficulty in refraining from singing. There were so many psalms suitable for expressing her gratitude and triumph.

She hoped they would all be at the manse, the minister, Elizabeth Greenloaning, Dora, and Edward Raitt, to see her, wee Agnes Tolmie whom they all pitied or laughed at, bringing home the spiritual remains of their wonderful Ann, demonstrator, rebuker of teachers, reformer of old women, and challenger of the Lord. She knew that Elizabeth considered her Old Testament kind of religion tasteless and absurd; perhaps the minister did too. She

57

knew Dora pitied her and Edward mocked her. Well, they would soon hear how their so well-brought-up Ann had gone to pieces in the first attack made on her personally by evil, and how on the contrary wee pluky thick-legged cranky Agnes had remained quite undaunted.

Edward Raitt's white car was at the manse door. He himself, dressed for golf, was putting in a corner of the lawn; in another corner Dora sat on a deck chair reading a magazine. He putted and she read so determinedly that Agnes saw at a glance, even before she'd got out of the car, that they'd been quarrelling. They were supposed to be playing golf that afternoon. A bag of clubs lay on the grass near Dora.

Seeing the car arrive, Edward, in the silly show-off way he'd always had, tried to balance a golf ball on top of his head. It fell to the ground before he'd noticed there was something wrong.

Dora noticed sooner. She threw down her magazine and running to the car opened the door, to look in horror at her sister seated there with Torch dead in her blood-stained lap.

"What's happened?" she wailed. "Was he run over?"

"I'm afraid not," said Agnes. "He was hit on the head with an iron bar by a young lout up the Bishop's Glen."

"Good heavens! Why?"

"Because they're vicious. They were pulling up some trees and Ann tried to stop them. So they hit the dog. Perhaps they didn't mean to kill him."

"And what were you doing?" asked Dora, of Luke.

"He was too far away to do anything," said Agnes. "Ann had gone ahead with the dog, you see."

Still in the car beside him, she put her hand on his thigh and pressed reassuringly.

By this time Edward had come over. He still had the putter in his hand, but when he saw the state Ann was in let it drop. About to show off as half a doctor, for that was all he was, he was roughly pushed out of the way by Dora who wasn't going to let anyone, not even him, perhaps at that moment especially not him, touch her sister. She helped Ann, as stiff as the dog almost, out. She pleaded with her, desperately, to put the dog down. Ann clutched it all the more closely.

"Better get her to bed," suggested Agnes. "She should be kept warm. She's had a shock. Phone for your doctor. Is your father in?"

"No. How can I get her to bed if she won't let go of the dog? Ann, please, put it down. Edward, take it from her."

But Ann refused to let him take it from her.

"Wait," said Agnes. "Let me."

She got out, with a last squeeze of Luke's thigh, and approached Ann.

"Come on, Ann," she said firmly. "Give him to me. I'll take care of him. You go with Dora."

To everybody's surprise, except Agnes's whose faith had never been stronger, Ann handed the dog over. Agnes took it without a flinch, though it was already stiff and stank a little of death.

"Look, Ann," she said, "we'll let him lie here for a while in the sunshine, beside the roses." She walked over to a deck chair and carefully laid the dog on it. She gave him a pat; it would help Ann if she was watching.

"Thank you, Agnes," called Dora, as she began to take Ann up the steps into the house.

"I'll phone for Monteith," cried Edward.

"Do it, then," said Agnes. "And if you know where Mr Plenderleith is, get in touch with him. Ann's had a bad shock."

In his grin dislike and condescension were mixed with admiration.

"Wee Aggie's come out of her shell," he said. "Am I going to have to admit there must be something in all that hob-nobbing with the Lord?"

"What you're going to have to do," she said, "after you've phoned, is to drive young Tommy there back to the Home, and Luke and me back to Bullwood Road."

He winked. "Are you and Luke living in sin there?" Then, laughing at his own lewd joke, he ran up the stairs.

Five minutes later, perhaps commanded by Dora to get rid of them as quick as possible, before the doctor came, he drove them in his car first to the Home where Tommy was left more or less on the doorstep—"He was born on one, didn't you know?" was Edward's little joke—and Agnes and Luke at Granny's gate.

"Thank you very much," said Agnes.

He grinned at her. "Is this you then arrived in the promised land? I like you in that red outfit, Aggie. It's real sexy. Cheerio."

He drove away laughing.

"Nothing's serious to him," said Agnes. "When he's a doctor he'll sign death certificates with a laugh."

Luke had his hand on the gate ready to push it open; she put her hand on his, with a pounce.

She noticed that her apron was still hanging on the hawthorn. Mick was gone. Perhaps that was why the blackbird and his brown mate that lived in Granny's garden were now darting about enjoying themselves.

"It's going to be different now, Luke," she said. "I mean, between you and me, between us," she added. "It's me you'll walk with," she went on. "We don't need a car. When I come into Granny's you'll not get up and leave."

"What about your father?" he asked hoarsely, not looking at her.

"Leave my father to me, and to my mother."

She reached up and touched his cheek. More daring, she reached up higher and kissed him, on the cheek. She hoped Granny was watching through the window. She didn't care if her father had seen. The sooner they,

and the whole world, saw her and Luke as sweethearts,
more or less engaged, the happier she would be.

Luke was trembling.

"Don't try to run away," she jested. "I'd be after you
with an iron bar."

She seized his hand to look at his wrist watch.

"Ten past five. I'll have to hurry. Be at the gate here
about half past seven when I'm on my way to my
dishes. In fact, Mr Dilworth, I'd be greatly honoured if
you would escort me there; and if you happened to be at
the hotel again about a quarter past ten it'd save Miss
Greenloaning having to send me home by car. I prefer
to walk. If we found the arrangement satisfactory we could
do it every night, except Sunday of course. In the meantime, cheerio."

Apron in hand, like a flag, she danced all the way
from his gate to hers. There was no danger from her
father: he was at the church repairing the roof. The Lord
was a hard master; even if you were not in His favour
you still had to serve. But if you were in His favour
how joyously and hopefully you could serve.

8

FOR THREE WEEKS Luke was Agnes's sweetheart. She
took him walks. She held his arm, she nestled close, she
gazed up into his face dotingly. On the esplanade and
even in the main street people passing who knew her
smirked: Agnes, they said, was as new-fangled as a wean
with its new rattle; others, more coarse, muttered it was
just as well she'd got hold of a jessie-wullocks, otherwise
she'd be in danger of getting bairned.

Her father several times threatened to pounce, but her
mother, with scorn like a tiger-tamer's whip, kept him
snarling in his corner. Agnes tried now and then, through
the bars, to soothe him with reassurances.

Acquaintances, father and mother, all would have been astounded had they seen her at work on Luke up the glen. Only the Lord would have understood that she was in her own way emulating Leah.

Not far from where Ann's dog had been killed tall bracken was growing. Luke was unwilling to lie down in it. She pushed him flat on his back. Then, while she tickled his nose with a stalk of grass, her left elbow hopped from his chest to his navel and then lower still. In the scuffle that followed she managed to unzip his trousers before he could wriggle clear.

Immediately she upbraided him for not finding her desirable, and then, increasing his bewilderment, for trying to take advantage of her. She pretended to sob. She said she wouldn't tell her father. She said that the only thing to do, if he was burning so hotly, was to get married.

He listened with his eyes wild with alarm and his hands placed where they could frustrate another attack on his zip.

Twice Elizabeth Greenloaning saw them together at the hotel. "It's very kind of you, Luke," she said, "to see Agnes home." She did not take them seriously as lovers.

There was one walk Luke went rather too willingly with her: this was to the manse to enquire about Ann, threatened with a nervous breakdown. They were invited in, but not allowed to see her: she didn't want to see anyone, explained Dora. But as far as Agnes was concerned the main purpose of the visit was achieved: the Plenderleiths saw them together like sweethearts. During the ten minutes in the house Agnes took care that her attitude towards Luke was amorous. She noticed that Dora was sorry for him, but the minister made up for it by constantly being on the point of blessing them both. From an upstairs window Ann watched them leave, arm in arm.

She took him to visit her mother while her father was away mending the church roof. It wasn't a success. Mrs

Tolmie wasn't enraptured with him. To his face she was polite but a bit dry and distant. Later to Agnes she was frank. "If he's really what you want, Agnes, I'll do what I can to see you get him. But don't rush into onything, take time to know him. To be honest, he struck me as a bit sleekit: I couldn't tell what he was thinking. You couldn't say he was very enthusiastic, could you? And he's too delicate, if you see what I mean, Agnes, no' delicate in the sense he's in bad health though he's hardly robust either, but delicate in the sense that—delicate's no' really the word I should be using ... I thought it was just your Uncle Archie's badmindedness, but he could be right."

"He's wrong."

"You seem awfully sure, Agnes. I hope you and this American—"

"I'm saying nothing, Mum."

"I don't like when you smile like that, Agnes. It reminds me you've always been more your faither's daughter than mine. Promise me you'll—"

"Shall we just say, Mum, that according to Deuteronomy I think it is Luke owes my father fifty shekels of silver."

"What's that supposed to mean? I'm no authority, like your faither."

"You'll find out, Mum."

"Agnes, why are you so sure this young man will have you?"

Agnes smiled the same sort of smile. It meant: because the Lord's behind me.

Her disillusionment therefore was all the more shattering when, on her last Saturday at the Arms—she was to take up a teaching appointment in lonely Glen Canach twenty miles from Ardhallow—Luke was waiting as usual at Granny's gate, but instead of fatalistically accepting her kiss he rudely turned his face away and said dourly, "I'm not going with you tonight. I'm finished. You've humiliated me enough. I don't want you. You've forced yourself on me."

She saw the blackbird and his mate, as beautiful and faithful as ever. The hawthorn was as green as ever, the gate as creaky, the sky as grey, Granny's curtains as lacy. Only Agnes's hopes were changed, calamitously.

"You daren't look at me when you say things like that," she whispered.

He pushed his face into hers. "I never thought I could hate anyone the way I hate you."

"You weren't so brave up the glen when the dog was killed, were you?"

He said nothing but showed his hate on his face.

She thought she saw Granny peeping out through the curtains.

"Does Granny know about this?" she asked.

"The old lady's known all along. She's advised me to get out of here, to go back to the ship. This is goodbye, Miss Tolmie. I wish I could be more friendly, but I can't. If I've hurt your feelings I'm sorry. I couldn't help it. For weeks I've been feeling desperate. Please don't ever pester me again."

Off he fled then, not into the house but round the back to the garden. At the foot was a wilderness of briers, brambles, and rhododendrons. She knew he often lurked there. He'd said he was watching birds. Now she knew he'd been gathering courage to make this attack on her.

Her legs shaky, she made her way to the hotel.

Had the Lord betrayed her? No, no, not betrayed; but had He, without consulting her, decided that Luke after all was not to be her sweetheart and husband? He should not have done. Divine and without limit Himself, He had this time overestimated her ability to endure disappointment. She did not know whether she loved Luke, but she knew she wanted and needed him. She had never been told what love was. Was it giving him her body to use as he

64

liked? But really it was his body she wished to make use of. Was it protecting him from others? But she wanted only to keep him in her power. Was it wanting to be in his company all the time? Any male company would have done, provided it was handsome and subservient enough.

All her life she had not been given a chance to learn what love was. Now when she was learning fast the lesson had been cruelly stopped.

Never before had she been afraid that the Lord in the end, in spite of His promises, would desert her. Having a doll or a bicycle withheld, though she had yearned for them for a long time, had only been disappointment, really a kind of guarantee that the ultimate gift, compensating for every deprivation from birth and before birth even, would one day be forthcoming. Now this Saturday evening, as she walked through the streets of her native town, in this dull weather so typical, passing people with faces as common as oranges and apples, not rare as pomegranates, she was afraid for the first time. In the gutter a piece of orange peel was just dirty orange peel, nothing more. The sense of wonder which had enabled her to see and feel and taste the presence of the Lord in every common thing was gone or suspended.

Had she been expecting too much to be done for her? Had she forgotten that the way to the promised land was not easy or free from pain?

9

AGNES'S MATES IN the washing-up squad were two widows, fat fortyish Bella with a randy laugh, and skinny sixty-year-old Hannah, who did not understand a quarter of her friend's bawdy remarks but tittered womanfully at them all the same. Both were under warning by Miss Greenloaning to respect young Agnes's religious upbringing and refrain from language likely to offend her. Being goodnatured, as well as sorry for Agnes because of that religious upbringing, they did their best to talk at "kirk level", though Bella couldn't resist now and then trying out some rollicking obscenity on Agnes, "juist to see if she turns green or something". To her surprise Agnes had remained unperturbed, though it was obvious that she had seen the dirtiness of the joke all right, even if she had seemed to miss its funniness.

It happened that that Saturday was Bella's birthday. She had been celebrating earlier and the smell of whisky on her breath was noticeable among the greasy soapy odours of the sink. She was indignant. She had "bumped into" her boss, Miss Greenloaning, who had told her off. So Bella now got revenge by indulging in some outrageous witticisms on the subject of her strait-laced employer and the latter's small-mouthed dog-collared fiancé.

"They say you can tell the size o' a woman's thing by the size o' her mooth," she said. "Weel, if the same's true o' men her ladyship on her wedding nicht's going to hae to pick it oot wi' a pin, like a whelk from its shell. God help her if there's a seagull aboot."

Hannah giggled but nudged Bella and winked towards Agnes.

"Hell, Hannah, Agnes isn't all that fond of our gracious mistress. Are you, Agnes?"

"No," said Agnes.

"You're awfu' quiet the night, Agnes? What's up? Don't tell me that pale-faced Yank's given you the heave."

Impressed by Bella's insight, Agnes wondered if she should consult her as a woman of the world, like the witch at Endor.

"Maybe it's her mither," whispered Hannah. "She's badly."

"Ach, so she is. I'm a forgetful pig. Sorry, Agnes."

"It isn't my mother."

"Is it the Yank?"

66

Agnes nodded. She was too depressed to lie.

"You're better off withoot him, hen," said Hannah. "These Yanks are no' to be trusted. Lead a lass to believe they're rich, then take her to a wooden shack we wouldn't keep pigs in."

Bella looked at Agnes seriously. "You're keen on him, aren't you?"

Again she nodded.

"I once knew a lass was going to be given the heave by a fellow she was struck on. She asked me how she could hold on to him. I asked her if he was the kind would marry her if he put her in the family way. She said he was. So I asked what was keeping her."

"Whit advice to gie a lass," muttered Hannah, shocked. "Did she?"

"She did."

"And was she put in the family way?"

"She was."

"You're making this up, Bella. Did he marry her?"

"He did not. It's true. He's paying for the wean to this day."

"You're no' suggesting Agnes should try it, Bella?"

"Agnes will try whit the Lord puts her up to," cried Bella, taking from her coat pocket her bottle of whisky, half full. "Let's droon our sorrows."

"Agnes cannae droon hers in whisky," said Hannah.

"Why not? It's a special occasion: it's my birthday, and she's been jilted."

"And this is my last night here," added Agnes.

"My God, Agnes, so it is. I forgot. Right, that settles it. You'll tak a wee dram wi' us. A cup o' kindness, as Rabbie said."

"Better make hers a wee one, Bella," said Hannah. "Enough to droon a flea."

"No," said Agnes, holding out her cup. "Drown a mouse, Bella."

Bella, with a yell of laughter, poured more than she'd intended. "Oh Christ, better let me take some of that back, Agnes."

"No."

"Your faither'll murder you, Agnes," said Hannah.

"To hell with her faither," cried Bella. "Well, here's to me; may I live to be a hundred."

Already disliking the smell, Agnes found the taste abhorrent, but she drank more deeply than they.

"Hold on there, Agnes," said Bella. "That's not water. Here's to you then, success in your new job."

"Thank you, Bella."

Again they drank.

"More, please," said Agnes.

"Right you are, Agnes," cried Bella. "After this, Agnes, you go to that Yank of yours and ask him what the hell he thinks he is giving you the heave, a lass born and bred in Ardhallow, a schoolteacher, and able, damn near, to recite the Bible from beginning to end."

"She's tiddly already, Bella," said Hannah. "I'm worried aboot her faither. You ken these holy kind, they believe in cruelty."

"We'll walk her hame, Hannah. The fresh air will sober her up. We'll buy her peppermints."

"Don't be concerned about me," said Agnes haughtily. "I can look after myself. I'll walk home, but alone."

Head spinning, she made shakily for the little lavatory outside the washing-up room. She shook off Hannah's attempt to help.

"You see, Bella," cried Hannah accusingly, "she's sick already."

But as well as sick, and dizzy, Agnes was also elated. She was not Agnes, she told herself, as she went in, snibbed the door, dropped her knickers to her feet, and sat on the pan, she was Leah, with the Lord's invisible hand on her back pushing her forward, towards what she could not yet see clearly, but she knew it must be fulfilment.

The Lord alone knew what desires, hopes, resentments, revenges and fancies clouded her mind then. Instead of pulling her knickers up again she found herself taking them off altogether and hiding them in a carton that had once contained packets of soap powder.

Light-headed and cool-loined she returned to wish Bella and Hannah good-night. With dignity she declined their offers to accompany her home, and waved away their advice to sneak into the house and get to bed before her father got a peep or a sniff at her.

"If you happen to see Miss Greenloaning," she said, "please inform her I won't be requiring her car tonight."

10

THE TOWN WAS fairy-lit. She walked along the sea front under coloured lights. In the water long bands of red and yellow and orange lights shimmered. Across the firth the lighthouse flashed. In the pier gardens two peacocks, one owl, and a cat, each outlined in fairy lights, roosted in the dark trees. The ruins of the ancient castle on the high rock above the pier were floodlit. The pier itself blazed like a ship.

Amidst all these illuminations were other radiances that only she saw. They could have been the suggestion of angels, but she did not insist that was what they were.

She approached the central part of the town. The pubs were closed but outside them American sailors in uniform and local youths were squabbling over and bargaining with girls, most of them frizzy-haired harsh-voiced prostitutes from Glasgow. Some were younger than Agnes but none more attractive.

There was one notorious alley between high blank walls, down which big Bella had said she wouldn't venture on a Saturday night unless she was wearing iron knickers.

It seemed sailors who couldn't wait dragged their whores there to use them against the wall.

Agnes found herself entering, terrified but still elated. Had the Lord Himself been standing at the entrance, instead of a drunk snarling obscenities, she could not have explained to Him why she was going home that way or what she hoped might happen. Perhaps she would have expected Him to know.

Halfway down the way was blocked by two sailors who stank of beer and whisky and two women who stank of cheap scent and gin. One of the latter was weeping viciously; the other was shrilly accusing one of the sailors of having cheated her friend out of some money.

Agnes had just squeezed past, with a timid "Excuse me, please", when another sailor, lounging against the wall and smoking a cigarette, put out his hand and caught her by the arm. Drawing her over to him, he sniffed the whisky off her, and immediately, stiff with hope, he peered into her face.

He had a drawl like Luke's. "Did he run out on you, honey? You're far too beautiful a girl to be left by yourself. What d'you say?"

She should have screamed and run. Instead, she stood still and silent as he put his hand on her bottom. She was horrified but also thrilled. She was getting her own back on Luke and at the same time getting even closer to him than she had ever been before. She thought of Leah creeping in the dark into Jacob's tent.

"You from Glasgow, honey?" he asked.

"I'm from Ardhallow."

"Local? I hope you live a long way from here, honey, for I sure would enjoy seeing you home."

She put her hand on his, to pull it away from her bottom which it was now hurting, but the thought occurred to her that this horrible but thrilling experience must surely have been arranged: this was her painful and

70

humbling way to fulfilment or the promised land.

She remembered Bella's story about the woman who'd tried to be made pregnant so that the man she loved would marry her. She also remembered the many lonely times when, making love to herself, she had begged the Lord to give her a lover so that she could make love in the way He approved. Now He had given her one in this dark smelly sinful alley, the kind of place He preferred to work His miracles in. By accepting and obeying she could make atonement for all those unlawful masturbations.

"Let's go, honey," he said.

As they passed some of his cronies these laughed and made lewd jokes; they called him Chuck.

"Don't you bother your pretty head with those dirty men," he said. "I'll take care of you."

His arm was round her. Luke's arm had been round her often, put there by herself. She began the pretence. This was Luke's arm, Luke's drawl, Luke's body.

She had to mention Luke's name.

"Who'd you say, honey?"

"Luke Dilworth."

"Yank, from the *Perseus*?"

"Yes."

"So it was Lukie let you down, honey? Can't say I know him. Evidently not a guy to be trusted. Now me, honey, I'm different. They'll all tell you that. I'm a guy that if he finds a genuine girl like you, why, he'll stick by her come snow come shit."

They were well out of the alley now. Under a lamp he stopped and took a long look at her face. She saw his: low-browed and heavy chinned, it could not be mistaken for Luke's. Yet weren't we all, the whole human race, in the magical hands of the Lord?

It was Agnes who chose their route. Therefore it was her doing that they took a path across a stretch of waste

71

ground outside Raitt's yard. It was covered with long coarse grass. People took their dogs there at night.

Again the sailor stopped her. From a friendly man reasonably gentle in his caresses he became a rough creature she didn't recognise, and was afraid of. Mumbling with lust he dragged her to a corner where no light from street lamp or window reached. His hand up her clothes paused, in joy, when it discovered she had no knickers on and was as ready for sex as he.

She could not have said whether she fell willingly or was flung down.

"That's it, honey, that's it, for God's sake," he muttered, as sprawling over her he tore her legs apart. "What difference does a face make? Christ, Christ, Christ."

He was trying, by no means gently, to thrust his big thing into her.

"Don't hurt me, Luke," she moaned, appalled by the pain in that place of pleasure.

To help her endure it she thought of Leah having to utter not so much as a sigh lest Jacob should discover she was not Rachel; and of Lot's daughters in the dark cave making him drunk so that he did not know it was into them he was putting his seed of copulation.

The sailor's prayer, for his reiteration of Christ's name was like a prayer, succeeded. Suddenly he was inside her, sliding in and out, bumping up and down. Stones in the grass pressed painfully into her back and buttocks. His gasps of encouragement could have been to a horse.

When he relaxed, with a groan half of pleasure and half of disappointment, she knew what had happened: he had ejaculated his seed into her. She could become pregnant.

For the next three or four minutes, as she looked up at the stars, faith deserted her. She was not any one special. She was only Agnes Tolmie who had been washing dishes that evening in Greenloaning's hotel. If she had a baby it would be a bastard without significance. She would be disgraced.

"Well, thanks, honey," said the sailor, as he got to his feet and fixed his dress. "You've got a lot to learn, but you set it up best you could."

He helped her to her feet but she immediately sank down again on her knees, whimpering.

He hesitated, willing to help but anxious not to get into trouble. "You all right, honey? You've not been long at the game, that's for sure. But I want to get the hell out of here. There's a stink of dogs' shit that's choking me. Here's something to pay the laundry bill, for if you've not got some dogs' shit on you somewhere I'm a Chinese acrobat."

He pressed a note into her hand and then hurried away, whistling.

She crouched there for another five minutes, while faith unaccountably returned. Her whole body felt bruised. Her "dainty" as Granny called it, felt torn and bleeding. She put her hand there and felt blood and also something thicker and stickier than blood: it smelled like dogs' dirt. The Bible called it the seed of copulation. It had to be washed off immediately with cold water; otherwise the Lord would be offended.

On her knees, aching, she prayed. The feeling of abandonment passed. She needed help now more than at any other time in her life. She would be given it. She would be told what to do; whatever it was she would do it humbly. In the end, no matter what other disappointments and suffering stood in the way, she would be granted happiness of a kind to make everyone wonder.

11

As she walked unsteadily homeward she felt as old as Genesis. Her mind was a jumble of stars, semen, pain, blood, Leah, dogs' dirt, Luke, and her father: over it,

73

darkly, moved the spirit of the Lord. Instead of these railings, these gardens with roses, these houses behind which people laughed at television, there should have been round her wide stony plains and black tents in which prophets with long beards waited for the Lord to speak.

Resting against the high stone wall that shut off Oliphant the lawyer's big house, she saw how, since the creation, the Lord had worked through imperfections, mysteries, and even evil. Otherwise everyone would be beautiful and good. Dogs' dirt would smell sweet as roses, or rather there would be no dirt of that kind at all, dogs' or birds' or animals' or humans', for bodies would have been fashioned to avoid pain and mess. What need then to find the Lord and worship Him? Therefore He had, for our own good, let disease happen, and ugliness, and death, and cruelty. He could have arranged the conception of children so that it was always dignified and beautiful. Instead He had left it so that it could be a greedy, callous, lustful squirting of semen, in long grass fouled with dogs' dirt. Yet, even then, what was the miraculous result? A human being, complete in almost every case to the pinkie nails, and containing intimations of the Lord and His inconceivable powers.

She reached her own gate, and was putting out her hand to open it when in her mind was born the desire, humble but urgent, to go along to Granny's and, simply by being near Luke, in some way possible to the Lord make a reality of the pretence that it had been he who in the darkness outside Raitt's yard had lain with her as Jacob had with Leah.

She opened Granny's gate quietly. The light was on in the living-room. Spurts of laughter came from the television. Creeping round to the back she found that Luke's room was dark. He must be watching television with Granny. Without really knowing why, she tried to lift up the window. She almost broke her finger nails but she

74

succeeded. The snib had not been mended. She left the window about a quarter of an inch open at the foot, just wide enough to let her fingers grip; again she did not know why. Afterwards she was to believe she must have been obeying instructions.

The window sill was low enough for her to sit on it and rest. After four or five minutes, however, she found herself creeping along the path to Granny's outside washing-house. It had a water tap in it. There, using her handkerchief, she washed herself with the cold water as well as she could, all the time looking to see if the light went on in Luke's room.

She was back resting on the sill for another five minutes before the light went on. She crouched down, and then, with immense caution, raised her head.

There was no blind. The curtains did not quite meet in the middle. Therefore she saw Luke from head to foot as he stood yawning in front of the dressing-table mirror. Her heart beat fast not only in fear of discovery but also in expectation. She had heard from Granny that he slept naked. She waited for him to undress. He took so long in starting that she began to be afraid he suspected she was keeking in. Then, within seconds, he was as bare as Adam.

If Agnes was fascinated by his spurtle, to use Granny's term so much less vulgar than others she knew, she was by no means more so than Luke seemed to be himself. Standing sideways to the mirror, he stared down at it and its reflection. Slowly it rose until it was as big and ready as Chuck's. She felt in no way horrified and disgusted, but pleased rather, and proud; as Leah must have been holding Jacob's.

Very tenderly, but even so more roughly than she would have done, he cupped the whole collection, the dark nest, the two eggs, and the great beaked bird, in his hand and dandled them lovingly for a minute or two.

Then, making her gasp, he let go in evident revulsion.

75

He switched on the bedside lamp and put out the overhead light. He picked up his Bible and rested it on his spurtle, until slowly this subsided.

She knew with loving intimacy what was going on in his mind. Often she too had used the Bible to try to overcome similar temptations. She hadn't always succeeded.

He got into bed and sat up reading the Bible, with a frown. His mind was still divided. His left hand was under the bedclothes.

Elsewhere in the house Granny could be heard moving about.

Behind Agnes, on the hill beyond the garden, a waukrife sheep bleated. It was a sound from Genesis.

Luke put the Bible down and switched out the light.

She was left staring in at darkness, and panting.

Then she acted, swiftly. A second before she had no thought of it. She was like one possessed or under divine goadings. Up she pushed the window, in she scrambled, off came her clothes, and she was down to only stockings and bra before Luke, with one weak yelp of astonishment, groped for the switch on the bed-lamp and found it.

Her bra dropped off. Her breasts, she thought, were like "young twin roes, her belly a heap of wheat set about with lilies". His eyes, though, were hardly as "the eyes of doves by the rivers of waters, washed with milk". They glared with shock, anger and desire.

Like those twin young roes of the Song of Solomon she skipped gladly to and into the bed, murmuring comfort and reassurance.

She put out the light.

Escape would not have been easy for him: he said afterwards he'd tried, she said he hadn't. Since the bed was against the wall his only way out was by the foot or over her. The tucked-in bedclothes blocked the first. He tried the second and was seized and held by her.

He did not then bellow or use his superior strength. Instead he went almost uncannily quiet and still, so that she was able, gently, to take hold of his spurtle and guide it into her. So limited her experience, she must have had unseen assistance for she succeeded very quickly.

"It's all right, my love," she whispered. moving to make him move. "Don't be frightened. I'll look after you."

That was the situation, he slobbering with resentment and lust, she murmuring loving encouragement as if to a child, when the door banged open, the light went on, and Granny, followed by Mick with his tail straight up, dashed in, in her pink flannel drawers and holding in her hand a big bread knife.

She could not believe what she saw. Mick, sniffing at Agnes's clothes on the floor, could not believe what he smelled. Both shrank back in horror.

"God Almighty," cried Granny, and pulled the bed-clothes off them. Luke in his position, face downwards, could do nothing to stop her. Agnes could but didn't. So Granny took a good look at them, "as scuddy as a pair of puddocks, in the act".

Her squeals of outrage were almost drowned by Mick's scandalised miaowings.

Granny sniffed. "No wonder you're complaining, Mick," she cried. "There's a dog been in here drinking whisky."

As clumsy as a sated puddock Luke crawled off Agnes, trying not to let Granny see either his face or his spurtle, both sunk in shame.

Granny's thin white hair was about her eyes. Her false teeth were in the tumbler in the bathroom.

"Get up, you shameless faggot," she said. "Take your claithes and go into my room. I've got something to say to you."

Agnes slipped out of bed, snatched up her clothes, and fled. As she passed Granny gave her a skelp on the behind, with as much affection in it as chastisement.

77

Luke still lay with his face turned away.

"Weel, whit's your story?" she asked.

"She came through the window."

"Were you expecting her?"

"No. I told you I finished with her this evening."

"So you said. But whit I saw twa minute ago was no' finish, lad, mair likely the start of something that could last a' your life. Why didn't you shout? Why didn't you coup her on to the floor? She's a sma' lassie, wi' half your strength."

"She took me by surprise."

She felt sorry for him. What had happened was clear enough, even if it was damned near incredible. Who would have thought Agnes could be so brazen, or Luke so guileless?

She felt all the more sympathetic towards him because in his inability to stand up for himself he reminded her of John Brisbane, a man easily cheated even at bowls.

Agnes was in the bathroom trying to wipe some marks off her skirt.

"Where did you get that?" asked Granny suspiciously.

"I sat on the grass in the pier gardens."

Granny snibbed the door.

"Agnes," she said, sitting on the lavatory for she was feeling exhausted, "you've taken a couple of years off my life."

"Don't worry, Granny. You'll be at our wedding."

"You as good as raped that boy."

"Granny, it's a physiological impossibility for a woman to rape a man. You should know that."

"Why the hell should I? Are you saying I've tried?"

The truth was, she had. Who was it had coaxed John McKenzie into her house, into her bed, into her, fifty years ago?

"Whit if you're pregnant?" she muttered.

78

"We'll get married. We'll get married whether I'm pregnant or not."

"Don't be so sure. Don't they say the worm can turn? I've the feeling, Agnes, you've found a victim. He's no' in love wi' you. And you, God help you, were never gi'en the chance to learn whit love between one human being and anither is. Whit's come over you? Up to a couple of months ago you wouldn't have told a lie to save your life. A' that good that was being saved up in you, has it been badness after a'?"

"I'll have to go, Granny."

"Your faither will be waiting for you wi' his belt."

"No, he won't. If he asks, I'll just tell him Miss Greenloaning kept me late to entertain me because it was my last night."

"So you're deceiving your faither as weel? Whit amazes me, Agnes, is that you can look so happy, as if you'd just done something grand, instead o' something mean and shameful."

"Granny, I once told you my time would come."

"Once? You've told me a thoosand times."

"Well, it's come now."

PART TWO

I

NOT MANY PEOPLE seeing Agnes Tolmie in the upstairs bedroom of Mrs McTeague's wooden forestry house
in Glen Canach, at twenty-seven minutes to nine on a
Wednesday morning in early October, would have guessed
that she thought herself the luckiest woman in Scotland. True, when she raised her head from the red chamber
pot into which she was retching and looked out of the
window, her glad watery eyes saw a sight as magnificent
as any in the country. An army of millions of evergreen
Sitka spruces marched up to the craggy tops of hills on
which the sun was just beginning to glitter. Much nearer
was the wide clear river where salmon glided behind
screens of brown and saffron leaves. During those pauses
too, as she listened, she heard the bleating of sheep, the
moaning of a wood dove, the far-off roaring of a stag, and
the laughter of children on their way to the small school
nearby where she was a teacher.

Though she appreciated them even at that time of stress,
it was not these splendours of nature that convinced her
she was favoured: it was because she was now sure she
was pregnant. She had had no period, and this was the
third morning she had been sick.

No one so far knew of her good fortune. She would tell
Luke, and her parents, when she went home at the week-
end. But as she spluttered into the pot, or glanced out at

the autumnal trees, or listened to the dove, she was reflecting shrewdly how and with whose help she would tell them. No one knew better than she that the Lord helped those who helped Him. So she had already decided to recruit as His agents her Uncle Archie and especially her Aunt Sadie. They would keep her father in check, and get rid of any foolish hankering Luke might still have at his last moment to deny responsibility and refuse to marry her.

Someone else, though, knew she was pregnant, but did not think it a matter for ecstatic congratulation. Indeed, her landlady, Mrs McTeague, was standing sadly outside her door, as she had been the previous morning too. Knuckles bunched against her big nose like its twin, the forestry worker's wife kept shaking her head and soughing in horror as she wondered how in Christ's name such a calamity could have happened to a girl protected by religion and also, it had to be said, by her lack of what McTeague himself had, too crudely perhaps, called cock appeal. Thickening the mystery too the cock that must have been enticed apparently belonged to the young American who brought her back from Ardhallow in a taxi on Sunday nights. From the glimpses they had got of him, he hadn't struck the McTeagues as an impetuous and irrepressible lover.

Still, as Mrs McTeague had reminded her husband, they had been wrong about Miss Tolmie herself when she had first arrived about six weeks ago.

Most of the people in the community had thought at first sight she was going to be even worse than Miss Proudfoot whom she was replacing. To everybody's surprise Miss Tolmie had proved a quick success.

She had a gaiety that at first disconcerted and displeased for it seemed so unjustified; she had far less to be gay about than most other folk, who nevertheless went about properly solemn. Soon, however, people began to laugh at the sheer unlikeliness of the small unbonny teacher as a joyous inspiration. They found they liked talking about her and hearing tales about her from their children.

The children thought her very funny, but to be laughed with, not at, like poor Miss Proudfoot. Laughter was often heard from her classroom, to the headmistress's instinctive disapproval. But when Miss Breckinridge after a fortnight examined Agnes's charges she found them remarkably eager and well up to the mark, even in spelling and arithmetic. To give Miss Breckinridge her due she had let everyone in the district know.

Mrs McTeague was about to knock and offer what help she could when the door opened and Agnes appeared, carrying the chamber wrapped in a towel. She looked as if she had been crying as well as vomiting, and Mrs McTeague's heart sank in sympathy. The poor girl would have the whole jing-bang against her: her holy tyrant of a father, the prudish Education Committee, and the Lord Himself. A teacher nowadays might enter a pub, if he was a man, and order a drink at the bar without losing his job, but no woman teacher, unmarried, however happy she was in her work, would be allowed to go on teaching if she became pregnant. It looked as if Miss Tolmie's career, started so well, was going to end so soon.

Perhaps Miss Breckinridge might be able to put in a good word for her. The trouble was, the headmistress's attitude to sex was equivocal. One day she'd make a joke that'd take even Molly McTeague's breath away, the next she'd be strait-laced enough to please the Free Kirk itself. There had been in the school playground a magnificent Scots pine, two hundred years old. Miss Breckinridge had it chopped down because it was decayed, liable to fall down in part or entirety in a gale and perhaps wipe out the total school population of twenty. But Mrs McTeague and one or two others had wondered if the real reason had been the squirrels which had flocked from all over the glen to mate in the ample lilac branches. Yet if you had asked Mrs McTeague to name any creatures able to make mating graceful enough to be respectable she would have said squirrels up a tree.

"I cannae tell you how sorry I am, Miss Tolmie," she said. "I heard you in there, vomiting, so I jaloused. What a hell of a thing to happen to a lass like you."

"What a heavenly thing, you mean," cried Miss Tolmie, laughing. "But you'll have to excuse me, or I'll be late. I suppose Donald and Douglas have already left?"

"Ten minutes ago."

Mrs McTeague felt weak as well as mystified. Could early pregnancy cause derangement of the mind, in a girl intoxicated by religion? Then she remembered her own two sons, dearer to her than the ten million trees outside were to the Forestry Commission, or the bombs down in Loch Hallow to the President of the United States. All right, having a wean was the most wonderful thing that could happen to a woman. But not to an unmarried teacher in Scotland, with a Bible-blinded father to be made to see reason, and a nervous Yank to be held to his promises.

She watched the cheerful rinsing of the chamber pot in the bathroom.

"Have you got it all planned then?" she asked. "Is he for taking you off to the States right away?" Before, she added to herself, they all get their claws into you here.

"Not just right away," cried Agnes, as she hurried back to her room, to comb her hair, and grab up her bag full of corrected exercises. Then she rushed downstairs, as happy as a squirrel in a pine tree. "He can't, you see. So we'll just have to get married here."

All that morning Mrs McTeague was to feel uneasy, surprised even by the taste of tea.

Though she had only a minute or two to spare Agnes

84

lingered on the bridge, with her chin on the soft green moss of the wall, gazing down to see if there were any big silvery fish in the dark brown water.

She thought of Luke with loving ruthlessness. During the past six weeks of their renewed courtship it had been evident that he was waiting to find out if she was really pregnant. Several times he had reprimanded her for being so confident and happy. He had even insinuated that her religion could not be sincere. It was quite probable that, with the desperation of a timid man, he would in a rage try to reject her and the child. This he must not be allowed to do, for his own sake as well as hers. They were both lonely. If they married they would be a comfort to each other. Much more important, it would please the Lord.

Whatever faint misgivings she had about Chuck immediately slipped back into the darknesses of her mind.

She was roused from this purposeful reverie by the ringing of the school bell. Running, she saw Miss Breckin-ridge standing by the door; the brass bell drooped in her hand. She looked uncertain and not very happy. She had been engaged to a man killed at Tobruk.

The children had already gone in. In Miss Breckin-ridge's room was disciplined silence, but in Agnes's they were singing with gusto, "Jesus Loves Me".

When the tall headmistress looked up and saw her small subordinate approach with that astounding and so far unaccountable happiness, she fixed her eyes on an isolated tree on a sunlit crag. She often gazed at it, to steady her mind. If she had had a frustrating experience with an unreachable child, such as Hamish McKendrick, or if she had been visited by one of her bouts of pessimism about her profession, she would look up at this tree in the blue sky and, most times, be calmed into sanity again.

Agnes Tolmie, though, that sanity could only begin

to cope with. Before the girl had arrived Elizabeth Green-loaning had telephoned to warn that she was very literal-minded, had no sense of humour, was rather sly, and above all was so old-fashioned that she still believed in Adam and Eve. Nevertheless, because of her bleak up-bringing, she deserved sympathy and encouragement.

From the very first day, however, Miss Tolmie had exhibited a rare, almost inspired self-confidence that Miss Breckinridge was at first inclined to rebuke as arrogance but as the days passed she could find no justification. Whatever its source, Miss Tolmie's joy had at once been communicated to the children in her charge, including the school's trouble-maker, Hamish McKendrick, who became too busy and happy to indulge in his spasms of mischief.

Miss Breckinridge knew that her assistant was in love: Miss Tolmie had told her so, several times. Perhaps that should have been sufficient explanation, but the head-mistress could not bring herself to think so. Love, of a sexual nature, made no one happy but the persons involved, and too often not these either. Only spiritual love, such as a saint's, springing from an instinctive and unshakeable belief in the goodness of God, influenced others. Miss Breckinridge was having great difficulty in seeing little Miss Tolmie from Ardhallow as saintly.

She shuddered, making the bell tinkle. Here in Glen Canach, hemmed in by trees, it was too easy for a lonely unfulfilled woman to find in this bright-eyed child or that, or hear in some mysterious sound in the forest, some closer intimation of the Lord than most of her fellow communicants in the Church of Scotland would have considered advisable. But if, in spite of that Calvinist caution, Miss Tolmie was to be seen as some such intimation, what was her purpose, what had she come here to reveal?

"You're late, Agnes," she said.

"Yes. I'm sorry. It's such a beautiful morning. I stopped

at the bridge to see if there were any salmon."

"I hardly think that's an excuse for being late."

But even as she said it Miss Breckinridge felt foolish and locked up in old, dark, backward ways. Five minutes stolen from mental arithmetic and spent on watching salmon in the river would benefit any teacher and therefore the children she taught. Better surely to share an appreciation of beauty than to pass on the ability to count and spell accurately. If it had been, say, an inspector fond of poetry telling her that, Miss Breckinridge would have been persuaded readily and gratefully, but to be beholden to, or instructed by, or, good heavens, inspired by this small, not very bonny, quite inexperienced daughter of a bigoted joiner was still too much for the headmistress's pride and scepticism.

"We don't get paid for looking at salmon," she said.

Agnes laughed. "Listen to them," she cried. "They're all out of tune." And she hurried in.

Alone again, Miss Breckinridge looked about her, at tree-stump, hills, trees, sky, and river, and listened to bell, birds, sheep, and children. It seemed to her everything was more in tune than ever. It must be that she had at last come to terms with her loneliness and disappointment. It could hardly be because of Agnes Tolmie.

2

MR DONALD MCCOLM, forester in Glen Canach, was a big long-nosed slow-witted plodding man from Jura, that island of Paps and soaring eagles. He did few good turns because, as all the men in the glen were under him, he felt that if he were particularly obliging to any one of them it would be bad for disciplining the others. This had given him a reputation for stupidity and meanness, but he thought no more of it than he did of a string of hoodie-crows strung up on a wire, to deter other hoodie-crows from what nobody ever asked.

On Friday afternoon at half past four he drew up in his Land Rover outside the McTeagues' house, to give Miss Tolmie a lift into Ardhallow. Angus McTeague, home early, watched from behind a curtain and was flummoxed by this unheard-of gallantry. He would have been even more flummoxed if he'd been told that McColm had no business to do in Ardhallow that evening, nothing to pick up at the pier, but was making the forty-mile journey there and back simply to accommodate Miss Tolmie.

Not naturally a mean man, and married to a kind-hearted woman from the more hospitable island of Islay, the forester had been waiting for years for someone to whom he could show kindness without being compromised professionally. Miss Tolmie was specially suitable as she wasn't bonny enough to stir up jealousy in his wife or ribaldry in his workmen. Besides, his seven-year-old daughter Sheila, hair soft as bog cotton, eyes blue as milkwort, was much slower at her lessons than the daughters of inferior men, and under Miss Tolmie an improvement had begun. McColm had come that evening primed to ask Miss Tolmie to give Sheila extra tuition, discreetly, so that no outsider need know.

Slow man though he was, the door of the Land Rover had hardly been slammed shut behind Agnes before he began speiring about Sheila's latest progress. Agnes answered honestly. Sheila's slowness, she explained, was not due to lack of ability so much as to a tendency to be too thorough. She would take as long over one sum as other children over six, but every figure would be meticulously executed and every line painstakingly drawn with a ruler. That the answer was more often than not incorrect was only to be expected after so much concentration.

"I'm a pit like that myself," he admitted. "Slow put sure. Always have peen, since I was a poy in Jura. My wife's the same," he added fondly. "You'll not find a more conscientious woman in Scotland."

Chary with praise to outsiders, like most Scotsmen, especially those from where the heather is thickest, he brooded for a good three minutes before muttering: "Sheila likes you, Miss Tolmie. She gets on well with you. We see a pig improvement."

"Sheila's really a very sensitive little girl," said Agnes. "She needs to have confidence in people. I'm glad she seems to have confidence in me."

After another three minutes he confessed that he and his wife had confidence in her too.

They were almost into Ardhallow, speeding along the desolate sea front, when they saw in the gloaming a boy with at least twenty big seagulls fluttering about his head. They seemed to be attacking him. Hacked by those strong beaks, his face could be a bloody mess.

Mr McColm stopped the Land Rover. Agnes leapt out and ran back. The gulls rose squeaking and squawking. The boy turned in surprise: his face was pale and unblemished. Her surprise was greater when she recognised him as Tommy Springburn.

"Tommy," she cried, "were those gulls attacking you?"

The birds had now settled on the rocks below, as if waiting for her to go away.

He shook his head. "They know me. I come here every night."

"By yourself?"

"Yes."

She remembered that when she had first seen him she had thought him a pauper pretending to be a prince. Now she saw she had been wrong. He was more distinguished than any prince. Like her, he was one of the chosen. Once she had had a beetle as a friend. She still confided in blackbirds. Through them she talked to the Lord. It must be the same with Tommy and his seagulls.

89

"Shouldn't you be having your tea?" she asked.

"I sometimes miss it."

Another sign: those closest to the Lord often forgot about food.

"Would you like us to take you home in the Land Rover?" she asked.

He hesitated, about to refuse. Then he nodded. She could have kissed him. He was like her brother.

Mr McColm at once agreed to drive up to the Home. He advised Tommy to carry a stick when walking alone near seagulls.

Agnes whispered into the forester's ear that Tommy was an orphan, with no people. Though she made it sound a distinction Mr McColm looked worried. He was always uneasy when he saw no connection.

"Mr McColm's the forester at Glen Canach, Tommy," she said. "There are lots of birds in his forest, including eagles. You must come and visit us."

"We'd pe very pleased to show you round," said Mr McColm, uneasily.

At the door of the Home, Agnes got out with Tommy. "Won't be long, Mr McColm," she whispered. "I'd like to have a word with Mrs Maxwell."

"No hurry, Miss Tolmie."

The door was unlocked. She opened it and went in, holding Tommy by the hand. The hall was empty and quiet, though a cheerful murmur of children could be heard elsewhere. Mrs Maxwell herself came forward, a stout motherly woman in a white cap. She shook her finger at Tommy.

"Late again," she said.

"I found him making friends with seagulls," said Agnes.

"I wish he would make friends with us. Off you go, Tommy. Wash your hands and then go to the dining-room."

He made for the stairs, with a smile at Agnes.

"How would you like to see my uncle's rabbits?" she called. "They're pedigree. They've won prizes."

"You're wasting your time, Agnes," said the matron.

But Tommy was nodding. "All right," he said.

"Good. I'll come for you tomorrow, about three. Is that all right, Mrs Maxwell?"

"Yes, of course."

They watched the boy go upstairs. Agnes waved, and he waved back.

"Well," said the matron, "if I hadn't seen that with my own eyes I wouldn't have believed it."

"Does he still not talk much?"

"He never talks at all. It's got so bad some of the smaller boys are afraid of him. He sits among them like a ghost. I'm sorry to say I'm thinking of asking to have him removed."

"He seems to like birds and animals."

"Except dogs."

Agnes remembered how he had shown no interest in Ann Plenderleith's dog, alive and dead.

"Because they remind him of people," added the matron. "That's a terrible thing to say, but I think it's true. If you could help at all, Agnes, I'd be more than grateful."

Agnes was now on the doorstep. "I'll do my best."

"I hear you're doing well in Glen Canach. I was talking to somebody from there, a Mrs McKendrick—she's got a boy in your class—and she was full of your praises. How's your mother, Agnes? I'm always going to pay her a visit but I never seem to find the time."

Mrs Maxwell's late husband had been Agnes's mother's cousin.

"She's going into hospital in a week or two, for an operation."

"I see. Well, let's hope it sets her right again. Good night, Agnes. I'll expect you at three tomorrow."

"Sorry, Mr McColm," said Agnes, as she climbed into the Land Rover. "Mrs Maxwell's worried about that boy. She's afraid he'll run away, I think."

"Why should he do that? It's a fine pig house. Is he a mental defective?"

"Oh, no. He's very intelligent. He's a foundling. Nobody ever claimed him."

Mr McColm thought of his little Sheila. Let her be at the bottom of every class, he would still love her and place her higher than any other child in the world.

"Good God," he muttered, at length.

After a long minute's pondering he added: "You're a good soul, Miss Tolmie, taking an interest in such a poy. It's not everypody that would."

3

IT WAS A jubilant Agnes that stood on the doorstep of Uncle Archie's small stone bungalow, rapping on the door with the bronze knocker shaped like a rabbit's head.

Holding a copy of that week's *Ardhallow Times* under his oxter, Uncle Archie opened the door. His red cardigan had bits of white rabbit fluff all over it.

"It's you, Agnes," he said, astonished. "Onything up? Is it your mither?"

From behind him came the dry sensible voice of his wife Sadie. "Why should there be anything up just because your niece happens to call? Come in, Agnes. If you were a rabbit he wouldn't keep you standing in the cold."

"It's not really cold, Aunt Sadie."

Agnes smiled. She should not have liked her Aunt Sadie, but she did. She was a confessed atheist, but she never laughed uselessly.

Outwardly Aunt Sadie was an ordinary, stooped, thin, careworn, working-class housewife of about fifty, with a firm mouth. Those who didn't know her pitied her being married to so stupid and contentious a man. Those who knew her well suspected she was the one who made the balls that so often exploded in the midst of the town council and made them regret foolish decisions. Archie was just the gomeril who fired them. She had once surprised Agnes by complaining that nothing exciting ever happened in Ardhallow. When the Americans had come with their submarines and bombs she had waited, so she said, for everybody to be blown sky high, or turned blue with radiation. When nothing happened she was contemptuous.

Uncle Archie, it seemed, had one of his famous letters in that week's *Times*. It was a diatribe against dog-owners who allowed their "slavering pets" to defile the town's pavements, "the narrowest in any civilised community". He was particularly proud of his last sentence. "If a rabbit can be trained, so can a dog."

Agnes dutifully read the letter and praised it for its relevance and correct grammar. She could have added a personal reminiscence supporting his theme, but did not.

"Not bad," he said, "for a man that left school at fourteen."

"That's enough, Archie," said his wife. "I'm pleased to see you looking so well, Agnes. I've never seen you look better; so happy too. Isn't Agnes looking well, Archie?"

He was again reading his letter, for the nineteenth time, Aunt Sadie said.

"I said, isn't Agnes looking well?" she repeated, sharply.

"She is. You're looking a treat, Agnes. Damn it, so you are. I could almost say you're getting bonny."

"A Scotsman's compliment," remarked Aunt Sadie. "So you're still liking it at Glen Canach?"

"Very much. I got a lift down in Mr McColm's Land Rover. He wants me to give his little girl Sheila extra lessons."

"Did he mention money?"

"No."

"Trust these Teuchters. Don't be like your faither, Agnes, obliging everybody and getting nothing in return, not even gratitude."

"I wouldn't like to take money for helping her. She's not very clever but she tries so hard."

"You've got something to tell us, Agnes. I see it in your eyes. They're sparkling. It must be good news."

Agnes laughed. "The best news in the world, Aunt Sadie. I'm going to have a baby."

Aunt Sadie instantly smiled, nodded, closed her eyes, and set her fingers dancing a furious reel on her lap.

Behind the newspaper Uncle Archie's face showed shock. His teeth became visible. According to his wife, when under stress he tried to look like one of his rabbits.

"Did I hear right?" he squealed. "Did she say a baby?"

"Well, she didn't say a rabbit," said his wife, whose fingers now, more relaxed, were dancing a strathspey. "This is a bit of news, Agnes, if it's true."

"In the war," muttered Uncle Archie, "when a man's heid was blown off not ten yards from me my knees never trembled the way they're trembling now. For God's sake, girl, you cannae mean it."

"She means it," said Aunt Sadie.

"But she's always reading the bloody Bible."

"What book contains more births? You're sure, Agnes?"

"Quite sure, Aunt Sadie."

"I didnae even think," mumbled Uncle Archie, "she kent how weans were got."

"Have you seen a doctor?" asked Aunt Sadie.

"Not yet."

"How often have you missed?"

"Twice. And I'm sick in the morning."

"God Almighty, Agnes," moaned her uncle, "whit have you been up to?"

"Don't you talk," said his wife, "you that sets rabbits

94

to breed that hate the sight of each other."

"Don't tell me," he yelped, "it was that peely-wally, wishy-washy, Yankee dreep that lodges wi' auld Brisbane did it?"

From Agnes's glad nod all that foolish disparagement of Luke had been deducted. She was noting too that the Lord was already hard at work in Aunt Sadie.

"So we're having a wedding soon," said her aunt.

"Yes."

"Don't be so sure," muttered her uncle. "These Yanks are famous for leaving bastards all over the world."

"Not Luke," said Agnes, smiling.

"Certainly not Luke," said Aunt Sadie, also smiling. "Does he know yet?"

"No."

"Then the sooner he does the better."

Uncle Archie groaned. "What's her faither going to say?"

"He'll be allowed to say a blessing," said Aunt Sadie, grimly. "Not a word else. We'll go there this very night and deal with him."

"We haven't had our tea yet."

"You'll get your fish fingers, Tolmie. Then we'll go with Agnes and complete some important business."

They went in the taxi, with its sign lit up. To Agnes's surprise, Aunt Sadie, who liked dignity, offered no objection. The three of them squeezed into the front, leaving the back empty for any passengers. These were most likely to be American sailors, in the main street. So that was the route they took.

Agnes remembered her promise to Tommy. "By the way, Uncle Archie," she said, "I promised to take a boy from the Home to see your rabbits tomorrow. Is that all right?"

"By God, Agnes," he muttered, in admiration, "you're

cool. Not many lassies in your predicament would be able to think o' rabbits, even mine."

As he spoke he braked. They were now in the main street. A sailor had come lurching off the pavement with his hand up. He had a friend propped against a lamp-post.

"They're too drunk," suggested Aunt Sadie.

"Double fare, Sadie."

The sailor poked in his head. He reeked of whisky. He was young and chubby-faced.

"Say, pop, could you take us to this address?"

Uncle Archie peered at the slip of paper. "This is an expensive destination, sailor."

"State your terms, you old pirate."

"Where is it, Archie?" whispered Aunt Sadie.

He whispered back, hoarsely.

"Thought as much." She tutted.

"It's a whorehouse," whispered the sailor, joining in the conspiracy. "Very private. Guy in the bar told us."

"Three pounds," said Uncle Archie. "I'm risking my licence taking you to a place like this. What about your pal? Can he manage?"

"Stevie's just resting. I'll handle him."

He made a quick faithful affectionate job of slapping Stevie awake, dragging him to the car, and pushing him in.

Uncle Archie drove off, chuckling.

"Me and Stevie, you see," said the young sailor, "took a fancy for a bit of tail. No harm in that."

"That remains to be seen," remarked Aunt Sadie.

For the first time he became fully aware of her, and of Agnes, as women.

"Beg your pardon, ma'm; and yours too, miss. Didn't notice you. You see, pop, this Scotch guy wrote it down for us. A new place he said. Safe. Clean."

Stevie made retching noises.

"I hope he's not going to be sick," said Uncle Archie. "A

drunk man's vomit lasts for months. It'll cost him ten quid."

"It was vodka did it. Would try vodka. Said if the Russkis could drink it so could he."

"If only the Russians could see him now," said Aunt Sadie.

"Stevie's all right. Awful homesick, that's all. The best of buddies. Gets pissed too easily."

"Language, please."

"Beg your pardon, ma'm. Yours too, miss."

They were now speeding along the dark sea front to the tiny suburb of Arnprior.

"Tell me," said Aunt Sadie, without turning her head, "do you happen to know a young fellow called Dilworth, Luke Dilworth? He's with the *Perseus*; works with radio."

"Sure. Can't say I know him exactly, but I've seen him around. Never drinks. Never smokes. Never cusses. Never visits whorehouses. Always asking Mr Stiegel, the chaplain, something."

"You make him sound like a very good clean-living young man."

"Oh sure. Skinny guy with a face like a priest. They put dirty pictures inside his Bible. For a laugh. Still, live and let live's what I say. If you're friends of his sorry if I've said anything out of place."

"Not at all," said Aunt Sadie. "You've been very helpful."

The car stopped. Agnes looked out. She was surprised. She knew the house, but she had no idea it was used as a brothel.

The young sailor dragged his friend out. They both looked ridiculously young and sadly far from home.

The taxi turned and went back to Ardhallow. The three pounds were in Aunt Sadie's purse.

Agnes was sorry they had taken more than three times

the right fare. It was all the greater pity this evening when they were in the Lord's service.

"Well, what did you think of that for a character reference?" asked Aunt Sadie.

"What I'm wondering is how a man as good-living as that could put ony girl in the family way, never mind Agnes."

"You stick to rabbits, Archie. You never were much of a judge of folk. This young man, that drunkards and whoremasters laugh at, is perfect as a husband for Agnes."

Aunt Sadie purred, like a cat, and patted Agnes's hand. Agnes, though, sensed a sharpness and necessary mercilessness, and was relieved.

In her mustard coat with grey fur at the collar and sleeves Aunt Sadie was more than ever cat-like as she walked stiff-legged up the path to Granny's cottage.

"It's a fine night," she murmured.

Stars gleamed in the sky, but far brighter were the two lighthouses flashing in the sea. Somewhere a dog barked. Ardhallow was at peace.

Uncle Archie knocked on the door.

"You're enjoying this, Sadie," he muttered. "We should be wearing sackcloth and ashes, and you're enjoying yourself."

"Agnes here has waited a long time for some happiness. I'm glad to be given the chance to see it's not taken away from her."

Luke opened the door. Mick the cat rubbed against his legs.

"Hello, Luke," said Agnes, sweetly. "It's me, Agnes. You know Aunt Sadie and Uncle Archie."

Scared, he was still polite. "How are you, ma'm? And you, sir?"

"May we come in?" asked Aunt Sadie. "Our business is too intimate to be done on a doorstep."

She led the way in.

As Agnes passed Luke she was sorry she couldn't give him the loving reassuring wifely smile she wanted to. Once his liberating ordeal was over all the love in the world would not be too good for him.

Seated by the fire, Granny was indignant at the invasion, as she called it. She did not look well: her face was as yellow and shrunken as a forgotten lemon.

"You always were a managing wee besom, Sadie Reid," she said. "Every game you played at, when you were a wean, you had to be the boss."

Aunt Sadie had turned off the television without waiting for permission.

"Now we can hear ourselves think," she said.

Ordered by her eyes, Uncle Archie took up his station by the door, to prevent Luke from escaping.

"And whit hae we to think aboot?" demanded Granny.

"Agnes is pregnant."

Luke let out a groan that amused Aunt Sadie, convinced Uncle Archie, and angered Granny. They did not know, as Agnes did, that he was undergoing the agony through which he would be liberated. They thought he was making a fuss because he had been caught.

"And you're responsible, Luke," said Aunt Sadie, "or should I say, the credit's yours?"

"Bugger you for an interfering bitch, Sadie Reid," yelled Granny in her anger. "Don't you daur snigger at that boy. He's worth ten of you."

"I was congratulating him on being about to marry the girl he loves."

"Loves, is it?" snapped Granny. "Don't be so damned sarcastic. You can see for yourself, whether he should or shouldnae, he doesn't want to marry her."

"He's got no option."

"He can always say no."

Uncle Archie had to intervene. "That's just what he

can't say," he cried. "Listen, young fellow. You'll be getting by far the best of the bargain. Agnes is educated, a trained teacher. And the Tolmies are a family wi' no mongrels: Scotch as far back as Bannockburn and proud of it."

Granny kept refusing to look at Agnes. "Pay no heed to them, Luke," she muttered. "Do whit your conscience tells you."

Luke then astonished them all. "If Agnes really is going to have a baby I'll marry her," he said, and then added the astonishing bit: "Poor Agnes."

"And what does that mean?" demanded Uncle Archie, full of suspicion.

"Shut your rabbity face," shouted Granny, who began to weep. "I'm too auld for this cairry-on." She took Luke's hand.

Agnes tried to take Granny's other hand, but the old woman turned away. Agnes sank down on her knees beside her.

"I love him, Granny. You know I do."

"I ken nothing of the kind."

"I'll make him a good wife."

Granny at last looked at her. "Sorry, Agnes, I cannae trust you. There's too much of your faither in you. I don't ken whit your game is. Do you ken yourself?"

Aunt Sadie rose. "Right, Agnes," she said. "Let's go and have it out with your father. Luke, you can see him later."

Agnes would have liked to go to Luke, to beg him to forgive her, and to promise that when this ordeal was over she would make it up to him; but it was too soon, his mind wasn't yet completely cleared of doubt, resentment, and above all hope that he might still escape.

As he held the gate open Uncle Archie muttered: "I don't like it, Sadie. What did he mean when he said 'Poor

Agnes'? We should have asked for an explanation. We ken nothing about him. He's a pig in a poke. There could be imbecility in his family, or worse."

"You go ahead, Archie," she said curtly. "Find out if he's in his workshop. We've got to be prepared."

He knew she was getting rid of him: she wanted to talk privately to Agnes. He had to obey. He had never admitted it to anyone and he intended to die without ever having admitted it, but he was really afraid of his small grey-haired wife. It wasn't a poker on the back of the head that he feared. It wasn't even her impatience with his stupidity. By nature an optimist, his innumerable failures had never made him lose faith in himself, and in the human race that he represented, he thought, as well as the next man. But his Sadie believed in nothing, certainly not in him.

He hurried on ahead.

"Right, Agnes," said Aunt Sadie, stopping on the road, "what did he mean with his 'Poor Agnes'? The wean *is* his?"

"If it's mine," replied Agnes, laughing, "it's bound to be his too. Don't you see?"

"I do not. Have you been to bed with him?"

"Yes."

"Where?"

"In his room, in Granny's."

"Why was she greeting then? I'd have thought, considering her reputation, she'd have laughed. And what was she on about asking what game you were playing? Does she know something I don't?"

"She caught us in bed together."

"Was that what she meant?"

"It must have been."

Aunt Sadie looked up at the stars. "It seems clear enough to me," she said at length. "How many times have I warned your father that the religion he stuffed into you every day wasn't healthy for a young girl? What book's got more incitement than the Bible? Daughters lying with their own father in a cave, women grabbing men by their stones. The first chance Agnes gets, I told your uncle, she'll take it. It was your father put you into that boy's bed and stripped you both naked and pushed your bellies together. So if he's going to do any ranting and raving he'd better do it against himself."

Agnes marvelled at how close to the truth Aunt Sadie had come: she had been put into Luke's bed, not by her father but by the Lord. Really that was what Aunt Sadie had meant; only, since she claimed not to believe in the Lord, she couldn't very well give Him the credit.

Uncle Archie was waiting for them at the door.

"He's in his workshop," he said. "Making something. I didn't go in. I just keeked through the window."

"It's a desk for me," said Agnes. "It's the first thing he's made for years."

"The next should be a cradle," said Aunt Sadie. "I see Isa's in her room. The light's on."

"Don't you think, Sadie, since he's in a peaceable sort of mood, you should leave the talking to me? You know you always provoke him."

"By telling him the truth? When did you ever get the better of an argument with him?"

"Well, if there is a God, and in spite of what you think, Sadie, there must be—how would we be alive otherwise, how would crops grow?—then Will, who's given a lot mair thought to the matter than you or me, 's mair likely to know."

"What good's it ever done him?"

"That's no' the point, Sadie."

"Be quiet. I want you to go to him, saying nothing at all, not a word, about why we're here, and, in about five minutes, bring him up to Isa's room where we'll be waiting for him."

"Is it an ambush? He's my brother after a'. And Agnes here has done wrang."

"Don't be a fool. Go. Mind now, not a word."

"Surely I'm to say she's here?"

"You can say that, but nothing else."

"You want to throw it at him like a bomb. Is that it? You're forgetting he's my brother. I used to sleep in the same bed wi' him."

"You're forgetting he's got a violent temper. You're forgetting he once gave Isa a bruise the size of a plum on her cheek. You're forgetting he almost killed a man."

"That was a long time ago, Sadie."

"In the past when they had power his kind burned folk at the stake."

In the dark Agnes smiled. Blaspheme how she might, Aunt Sadie was nevertheless obediently doing the Lord's will.

"Why are you so quiet, Agnes?" asked her uncle. "Aren't you going to speak up for your faither? You used to be fond of him."

"I still am."

Aunt Sadie let out her breath slowly, in a long deliberate sigh. "So you should be, Agnes," she said at length. "He's still your father. But, Agnes, if you shame me in front of him by going doon on your knees and begging him to forgive you I warn you I'll walk right out and leave him to chastise you as he thinks fit."

"I'll go down on my knees only to thank him for forgiving me."

Aunt Sadie considered that. "Very well. I'd go doon on my knees to no man, but you were born on yours more or less. If he accepts the situation, with good enough grace, you can thank him any way you please. Are you going, Archie?"

"I'm going," he grumbled, and went.

Aunt Sadie and Agnes went into the house. Agnes had a key.

"It's me, Mum," she called up the stairs. "Aunt Sadie's with me."

They began to go up.

"Your faither's in his workshop, Agnes," called her mother. "He's still working at your desk. He's going to finish it."

She was in bed, combing her hair. She looked very ill but glad to see them.

"I was wondering if you'd manage doon the night, Agnes," she said, smiling. "It's nice to see you, Sadie."

"I got a lift down in Mr McColm's Land Rover, Mum."

"Imagine that now. They think the world of her up there, Sadie. I got a letter from the headmistress."

"I saw it, Isa."

"From what I hear she's not the woman to give praise where it's not due. All the same, Agnes, I still would like you to get a job nearer hame."

Aunt Sadie had sat down in the only chair in the bedroom.

"There are going to be changes, Isa."

"Changes? What kind of changes, Sadie?"

"Prepare for a shock, Isa."

The sick woman tried to laugh. "I don't think I'm fit to bear a shock, Sadie."

"Even if it's a shock of happiness, as it should be?"

"Happiness? Aye, I could bear that."

"Look at Agnes, Isa. She looks happy, doesn't she?"

Mrs Tolmie smiled in tears at her daughter.

"She deserves it," she said. "She's waited long enough."

"She's going to have a baby, Isa."

The comb stopped. Mrs Tolmie looked as if she was saluting; but on her tired face dismay slowly displaced incredulity.

"You're joking, Sadie."

"If anybody's joking, Isa, it must be Agnes. She told me and I believed her. There she is. Ask her."

Agnes sat on the edge of the bed and took her mother's hand.

"It's true, Mum."

"You mean, you and Luke ... ?"

"Yes, Mum, me and Luke. Don't worry. It's all right. We're going to get married."

"They are," confirmed Aunt Sadie.

"Your faither will murder you," wailed Mrs Tolmie.

"He might try," said Aunt Sadie. "That's what I'm here for, to prevent it. Archie's here. He's bringing Will up in a minute or two. We're going to discuss it quietly and sensibly, as a family should. We're going to put first things first, and the very first is Agnes's happiness. You agree with that, Isa?"

"Of course, Sadie, but you don't know what this'll do to him."

"Make him more human, I should think."

"It'll hurt him to the he'rt."

"I don't suppose any father would rejoice to hear his unmarried daughter's pregnant."

"You don't understand, Sadie. He'll think, you see, everything he's believed in has turned out a mockery. It'll kill him."

"Isa, is it only him you've got concern for? Are you aware you've said nothing to Agnes, not one word of encouragement?"

Mrs Tolmie looked at Agnes. "You should have waited, Agnes. It's a disgrace in any family; worse in ours. You should have waited. You've just been working six weeks. And I'm not sure either I care very much for him, Luke I mean. You should have waited."

"Well, she didn't, Isa, so that's that. Look on the bright side. Agnes will get married. She'll go to America more than likely. You can go with her. And you'll have your grand-wean to look after."

"We'd be delighted to have you, Mum," said Agnes.

"You ken I couldn't leave your faither."

"Isa," said Sadie sternly, "I've heard you say a hundred times you were minded to leave him."

"I never meant it."

Then they heard the back door downstairs opening, and voices; even laughter.

"Maybe he's taking it calmly," whispered Mrs Tolmie. "I pray to God he is."

"He doesn't know yet," said Sadie. "I warned Archie not to tell him. You know what a blunderer Archie is with news."

The two brothers were now coming up the stairs. It was Agnes's father who was laughing.

Agnes then did what she knew she should never do, what she had been taught always to avoid: that was, put the Lord at risk. She prayed that Aunt Sadie would speak kindly, that her father after reproaching her would forgive and bless her; that her mother would recover good health after the operation; that she and Luke would get married soon; that their baby would be beautiful; that, so overflowingly happy would they be as a family, they would take Tommy Springburn to live with them.

The Lord could have granted all that, for His powers were without limit; but if He chose not to it would be for reasons of His own, not to be questioned. That was the centre-stone of faith.

At first she thought, her heart beating fast, that it was going to happen. Still in his brown overall, and stooped because of his now chronically sore back, her father was as peaceful as she had seen him for years. She knew him so well that she could detect in his grave smiles tremors of pain that Aunt Sadie certainly didn't notice. Deeper still, but detected by her was the abiding pain of

106

knowing that his service to God, which must be continued, was not to be rewarded, either in this life or the next. Agnes had once tried to persuade him that perhaps his view of his prospects was too pessimistic, it presupposed in the Lord an eternal hardening of heart. With remarkable calmness for a man doomed to all eternity he had said the Almighty's judgements must not be questioned. He had added, after a long prayerful pause, that he might have one chance. If Agnes, his daughter, reared by him from birth to honour the Lord, won favour in the eyes of the Lord then he, her father, might, out of the Lord's mercy, be received back into the fold.

He would say now she had been guilty of fornication and unlawful conception. He would never believe the Lord had abetted her. He would think, so wrongly, that she, more surely than he, was damned.

Aunt Sadie was fidgeting with impatience. The right moment for her to throw the bomb was too long in coming. Her victim seemed too reasonable, too meek, too fond of his daughter, too likely therefore not to be shattered at all.

When she did throw it she was awkward, her aim wasn't as cool and accurate as she'd planned.

"You'll be wondering what's brought Archie and me here."

"You're always welcome, Sadie."

"I can mind the time when you rose up and walked out when I came."

"Admit it, Sadie," muttered her husband, "you were too savage against religion in those days."

"If I was ever rude to you, Sadie," said her brother-in-law, "I'm sorry."

"Rudeness is nothing compaired with cruelty, Will. You cannae deny you've been cruel many a time to Isa and Agnes." Her voice rose. "You've kept them apart, Agnes especially. You made her different from other girls, deliberately. You even grudged her dolls to play with. Pleasure was sinful, you taught her. Other weans would run dancing on a Saturday to the shop for a new comic or sweeties. Never Agnes. She'd to stay at home and read the Bible."

"This is past history, Sadie," muttered her husband.

"Is it?" she yelled. "Then I'll give you present history, not to mention future history. You're still managing to look humble, Will. Let's see if it's more than skin deep. Agnes there, your only daughter, Will, your offering to the Lord, Will, is going to have a baby. Aye, Will, a baby, same as your Virgin Mary had, if you remember. So you're going to be a grandfather, Will, which is more than your brother ever will be."

She ended in tears she couldn't stop, however she resented them.

Agnes saw on her father's face first blankness, that persisted, as if he was never going to understand; then, very briefly, pity, but whether for himself or her she couldn't tell; then astonishment that couldn't be kept out; then sorrow, and joining with it slowly revulsion that deepened and deepened until she saw it possessing his whole soul.

"Is this true?" he asked, his eyes closed.

No one was sure who would answer.

"Am I a liar?" cried Aunt Sadie, shrilly.

"Aye, Will, it seems to be true enough," said Uncle Archie, "but it's not the end of the world."

"Don't take it so bad, Will," whimpered his wife. "Sadie's right, you know: you never gave Agnes the chance to take to life naturally."

"Yes, Father, it's true," said Agnes.

It was her he heard. He took a step towards her. Aunt Sadie rushed between.

"Keep your hands off her, Will Tolmie," she screamed.

"No violence, Will," urged his brother. "For God's sake it's not the end of the world. Nobody kens but us. She can be married at once. There will be nae disgrace."

Held back by his brother, opposed by his sister-in-law, and wailed at by his wife, the stooped, bald joiner ignored them all and held out his hands to Agnes.

"Is it true?" he repeated.

"Yes, Father, it is."

"Then I don't want ever to see your face again."

He shook off his brother's grip and went out. They listened to him going down the stairs.

"He means it," cried his wife. "He'll never forgive her, this side of the grave."

Nor the other side either, thought Agnes with a shiver.

"He'll come roon'," muttered Uncle Archie.

"It's as well I asked you to leave your things at our house, Agnes," said Aunt Sadie. "You'd better stay with us till we know it's safe. Archie will tell you, I've always said religion did more harm than good. If you want to find somebody doesn't know the meaning of forgiveness, go to a man of God."

Agnes tried to comfort her mother who was weeping. She did not know herself what the next move should be. It was one of those situations when the Lord had to be trusted to act for Himself.

4

THE REVEREND HARRY L. Stiegel, aged thirty-seven, Baptist from Idaho, chaplain attached to the U.S.S. *Perseus*, was an enthustiastic optimist. Formerly on the football field the most fervent and friendly dislocator of bones, he was convinced and dared to say it publicly that the H-bombs under his apostolic jurisdiction, as he put it himself, each one capable of destroying an entire city, would never dislodge so much as a single brick. To display his confidence in the Christian purpose of those bombs he had a great Cross in lights erected on the ship at Christmas.

That half the neighbourhood was affronted by no means discouraged him.

Not many of the men came to his services. Only one, out of hundreds, had ever consulted him as to the morality of a Christian being involved with the bombs. This was young Luke Dilworth. To him Mr Stiegel had enthusiastically pointed out that today, in this age of rockets that flew at the rate of thousands of miles an hour, faith itself had to be streamlined and swift, with its own explosive warhead. This did not make a great deal of sense when repeated afterwards to his friends Robert Plenderleith and Elizabeth Greenloaning in the former's manse, but it impressed Luke who was, after all, a simple boy from a town with beliefs primitive even for rural America.

Though he had three children under five, the youngest, Baby John, just ten months, Mr Stiegel's wife Trixie, blonde and buxom, took such a busy part in all the social activities of the officers' wives that he was often left to baby-sit; which was how he was occupied one cold wet windy night when Luke paid him a surprise visit.

When the bell rang Mr Stiegel did not hesitate to throw the door open, with welcome ready on his lips for the caller whoever this might be, whether some Scotch kid collecting for a local charity, or Captain Steveley himself. He was clutching Baby John who stank, though Mr Stiegel, having been with the smell since its beginning in the hot stuffy house, was not so keenly aware of it as a newcomer out of the fresh air must be.

Two-year-old Sis Sue, with jam all over her pale face and paler hair, clung to his leg. Behind him, Harry Junior, aged four and a half, bow-tied, with the assurance of the first-born, was tapping the handsome wood panelling of the hall with a hammer so heavy he had to hold it in both hands, as Japanese officers did their swords of execution.

At first Mr Stiegel was not sure who the rating was,

with his coat collar up about his ears and his cap pulled low; but he recognised the voice that, bless it, would still have been solemn and respectful if his chaplain, the Lord forbid, had come to the door as naked as an ape.

"I'm sorry, sir, if my visit's inconvenient. You said if we had any private problem—but if it's not convenient I'll drop by another time."

Mr Stiegel put out a big hand and caught the young man by his soaked shoulder.

"Of course it's convenient, sailor. You've come through the night with your problem, whatever it is, and I'm here, ready with sympathy sure thing, and perhaps, who knows, with wisdom too, if the good Lord sees fit to assist. I hope you don't mind the children. Where little children are present, Luke, the good Lord's never far away."

He saw his visitor glance anxiously at Harry Junior who was now hitting the wall with more force than the old lady who owned the house might have approved. Still, there were already so many small indentations—Trixie too, bless her, believed in letting the children find their souls by doing—that a few more were hardly worth fussing about.

"Better take that wet coat off, Luke."

"It's all right, sir. I won't be staying long."

"Stay till midnight, fellow, if it's necessary."

The invitation, though warmly expressed, was not quite sincere. Back from her Women of the Protestant Chapel meeting, Trixie would not be pleased to find young Dilworth there. She had been present at the manse when Luke's friendship with Miss Ann Plenderleith had been discussed some time back. She had declared trenchantly that while she might manage a little sympathy for the daughter of a Christian minister, especially a Scotch one, who protested against the Bomb, she could manage none at all for an American sailor who had sworn an oath of loyalty.

Mr Stiegel assumed it was still the same sore on his conscience which was troubling Luke: he had come for some more Christian salve, robustly applied.

"Tell you the truth, Luke," he said, as he showed him into the living-room, "I'm glad of a little adult company. Children are the Lord's favourites, how true, but they sure can monopolise a man's attention."

A chamber pot, with contents, sat on the carpet, easy to see and trip over. Round it were dozens of toy soldiers, most of them beheaded, a model yacht with dishevelled red sails, a doll with an arm missing, and a small drum with the stars and stripes round it.

There was a huge sofa and two big clumsy armchairs, covered in bilious yellow; they were grimy too, as was the high corniced ceiling, with smoke from two oil heaters. The room was very hot. Trixie would complain otherwise. By her orders the windows were closed, with heavy velvet curtains drawn, also grimy yellow.

Little Sue, not feeling well, began to fret. She held her head.

"What's the matter now, honey?" asked her father, with a sigh.

"I'm afraid, sir," murmured Luke, "the little boy hit her on the head with the hammer."

What a priggish utterance from a sailor in the U.S. navy, thought Mr Stiegel. The poor fellow must have had very backward religious mentors. He was so obviously confused about right and wrong, and lacked the verve and elasticity of the truly modern Christian.

"Oh, he was only in fun," he said. "The little man adores his sister."

Sis Sue, though, interpreted Luke's remark differently. She heard sympathy in it. So over to Luke she waddled and, hampered by her sodden diapers that trailed, clambered up on to his knees. Those, as her father reflected happily, were themselves already sodden, with rain, and so Luke would scarcely notice any extra discomfort. She wasn't content just to sit on that wet lap, safe from Harry Junior, not Sue, that subtle little woman of two and three months. She fussed and whined until Luke put his arms round her. Then, head nestled against his breast, she went off into her peculiarly snorting sleep, caused, Dr Schnepf had recently told them, by enlarged adenoids.

Mr Stiegel himself had the more demanding burden. Baby John was at the slavering stage, and he loved to dance on his father's knees, steadying himself by grabbing at his father's hair which gave no grip, and at his nose which did, but painfully so.

Somewhere in the background Harry Junior was tapping on the glass door of a bookcase, with a restraint equalled by his father's. Mr Stiegel felt, as a conscientious tenant, he ought to confiscate that hammer, but he also felt, as an intelligent parent, that his son ought to be given opportunity to do some damage so that he could later on in his development enjoy the triumph of deciding not to do any. Civilised people, Mr Stiegel would tell you, were merely reformed vandals.

"Well, Luke," said the chaplain, "now we're more or less settled, is that conscience of yours still on the wrong wave-length?"

"It's not that, sir."

Yet he was looking as ill at ease as anyone with as raw and callow a conscience as his might be expected to look. He seemed almost unwilling to breathe. Suddenly it occurred to Mr Stiegel that there might be, indeed undoubtedly was, a stink in the room. That pot, for God's sake, ought to have been taken away and emptied. Still, might it not do this too morally fastidious young man good to be reminded of man's animal nature?

"Then what is it? Not trouble at home, I hope?"

"No, sir."

"Glad to hear that, Luke. I'm sure you have a wonderful family. What is it, then?"

"Mr Stiegel, sir, I want to know would it be wrong for a Christian to marry a girl he doesn't really love, couldn't ever love, just because she's in trouble and needs help?"

At that moment Harry Junior succeeded in hitting the glass of the bookcase as hard as anyone could without shattering it. His father, pummelled by Baby John, turned round not to rebuke his heir but to suggest to him he might be happier playing with his toy soldiers. Sis Sue was asleep, he said; surely Harry didn't want to wake up his little sister, who wasn't well.

Harry Junior replied frankly that he didn't care whether he woke up his little sister or not.

Mr Stiegel laughed, as if at some minor triumph, took Baby John's fist out of his eye, and returned to Luke.

"Now, Luke, please, for Paul Jones's sake, no generalities. This Christian, he's you, isn't he?"

Then he realised, with broadminded amusement, that what Luke seemed to be confessing to was having got some girl with child. It was so unlikely and interesting an occurrence Mr Stiegel wished he was free to take an anthropologist's interest in it, instead of a padre's.

"Who is this girl you've got in trouble, Luke?"

A foolish fear struck Mr Stiegel then. "Not Miss Ann Plenderleith, for God's sake?"

Luke frowned huffishly. "No, sir. Of course not. I haven't seen Miss Ann for weeks."

"Have the advantage over you there, boy. Saw her last week."

"How is she, sir?"

"Ah yes, how is she."

Mr Stiegel found it difficult or at least awkward to say how Ann was. Several people had asked him, including Captain Stevely. Trixie's own diagnosis was that Miss Ann's breakdown, if it could be called that, had as its purpose the postponement, perhaps even the total cancellation, of her father's marriage with Elizabeth Greenloaning. Trixie maintained that in her heart Elizabeth shared this view.

Ann's father, however, an admirable minister, and her sister, a beautiful and level-headed girl, seemed to think that what Ann was suffering from was no less than the eclipse of Christian hope. She was convinced, they said, that if not in ten years or in twenty then in fifty, the human race would destroy itself in a nuclear Armageddon. Moreover, she was glad this was going to happen. She was ashamed of being human.

All the same it was difficult in words to make credible or convincing or worthy of solemn sympathy such a malady in a girl of eighteen. Certainly the doctor was treating her, and a specialist had been summoned from Glasgow. But did not medical men come because they were sent for, not always because they were needed?

"I was with her, sir, when her dog was killed."

"So you were, Luke. I had forgotten."

But Mr Stiegel decided these waters were too murky, dangerous with hidden rocks, so he put about.

"Let's get back to this girl you've got in trouble," he said. "By trouble I assume you mean she's pregnant?"

Luke hung his head. It wasn't all that easy to distinguish his shamed gasps from Sis Sue's snuffles.

"Yes, sir," he whispered.

"And she says you're to blame, is that it?"

Luke looked up, mouth open. Either he scented hope, or the stuffiness of the room was clogging his nostrils.

"Yes, sir," he snuffled.

"With that type of woman, Luke, it's hard to say who's to blame. It could be one of fifty. But let's establish your share of the culpability. Did you have relations with her? Let me use sailors' language. Did you have your penis in her, boy?"

It wasn't really very sailorly language. He could think of no sailor, from cook to captain, who would have said penis.

"Yes, sir," admitted Luke, with another snuffle.

Mr Stiegel winced, but it was because there came then, from the swank sitting-room, a loud crash.

"Well," he said bitterly, "isn't that what whores are for?"

"She's not a whore, sir. She's an Ardhallow girl."

"Are you telling me Ardhallow girls can't be whores? Did you pay her?"

"No, sir. You've got it wrong, sir. She's not that kind of girl at all."

"Look, sailor, she let you fuck her, didn't she?"

He was rather proud of having at last used real sailors' language. Therefore he wasn't pleased when Luke went coy and seemed not to be sure after all. Trust you, thought the chaplain, not to be sure where your cock has been.

"Has she got a name?" he asked.

"Yes, sir."

"What is it?"

"Agnes Tolmie."

"Agnes Tolmie?"

Just then Harry Junior began to bawl; even his stout heart quailed at the damage he had done. At the same time the noise of Trixie's Dodge was heard outside. She wouldn't be pleased to find in the house a sailor come to complain about being blackmailed by some amateur whore. Better therefore in the meantime to pack Luke off and see him on the ship tomorrow.

He rose. "Well, here's my sweet lady," he said cheerfully.

Baby John seemed to know his mother had arrived: he set up a howl of pre-welcome. Harry Junior, still bawling, was already at the door, to make sure he was cocooned in motherly love before the shattered cabinet was discovered.

Sis Sue, in Luke's arms, slept and snuffled.

"See you on the ship tomorrow, Luke," whispered Mr Stiegel. "But let me give you this much comfort. Not even in Scotland would a court make a man marry a whore."

In then, screaming maternal comfort to Harry Junior, dashed Trixie. She gasped at seeing her daughter in the arms of a sailor she suspected of being some kind of pervert. But she always remembered she was a minister's wife.

"Why, Mr Dilworth, this is a surprise. What an awful night for a visit. It's a pity you're going so soon."

Relieved of Sis Sue, who parted from him with whimpers of dismay, Luke took his departure promptly. He was not quite quick enough out of the door to avoid hearing Mrs Stiegel cry, in her brassiest voice, "What did that creep want?"

It was a question her husband did not feel able to answer candidly. A Protestant minister was every bit as much under a sacred obligation as a Catholic priest not to betray confidences. No Catholic priest, however, had a wife with a tongue as relentless as an ant-eater's at digging out tasty information.

"I wouldn't call him that, my dear," he said.

"Is it still that rubbish about his Christian conscience?"

"Yes, but in a personal matter."

"I don't believe a creep like that's got any personal life at all."

"You'd be surprised, my dear."

"Don't snigger, Harry. It doesn't become you. What would surprise me?"

"I'm not at liberty to tell you that, Trixie. It would not be ethical."

"Am I your wife, Harry Stiegel, or your unpaid help?"

That was a question she frequently yelled, this time in her hardest, most belligerent voice. The meeting of the Women of the Protestant Chapel must have been disputatious: Trixie had not got her way.

It was of course a rhetorical question. In the past he had made the mistake of trying to answer it earnestly, only to find that his most passionate protestations of love and loyalty infuriated her still more. Now he merely stood, head bowed, hands clasped, shoulders back, in a posture not too clerical, with something of a sailor's honourable surrender in it...

About half an hour later while Trixie was upstairs bathing and bedding the children, from which rite she had barred him, he slunk into his study where he rang up Elizabeth Greenloaning at the hotel. As an oracle on Ardhallow affairs she was much more useful than her fiancé. Mr Stiegel was sure that Robert Plenderleith often in private reveries saw himself as the man who would reveal to the world the formula by which its incorrigible wickedness and the love of God would be reconciled. Elizabeth once, in Mr Stiegel's hearing, had gently but formidably pointed out to her fiancé that if millions were killed by H-bombs in some future war, the love of God, though never absent, none the less did not come into it. She was a Christian without a qualm.

It was reassuring just to hear her voice, quiet, euphonious—since coming to Europe Mr Stiegel had discovered that American women, including his Trixie, had grating voices—and Scotch enough to give it flavour without loss of intelligibility.

"Elizabeth Greenloaning, Ardhallow Arms," she said.

She had an exquisitely furnished eyrie of a flat at the top of the hotel, with an inspiring view of the firth.

"Good evening, Elizabeth. Harry Stiegel here. Sorry to bother you at this time of night."

"No bother, Harry. Glad to hear from you at any time. How are you? And Trixie? And the children?"

"Poor Sis Sue has a touch of diarrhoea; otherwise we're in excellent health, praise the Lord. And how are yourself, and Robert, and Miss Ann?"

A slight pause. Had Trixie been there she would have given him a blue-lidded wink.

Still, the pause could merely indicate natural reluctance to talk about a young girl sunk into depression.

"We had her out for a car run today."

"Beginning to take an interest in things again? How glad I am to hear that, Elizabeth. Our prayers have been answered."

"Not quite, I'm afraid. She still, it seems, wakes up at night and weeps. Well, Harry, is there anything I can do for you?"

"Well yes, there is. I've just had a surprise visit from our young friend Luke Dilworth."

"Oh. I'm afraid I haven't seen anything of him for weeks. How is he?"

"In a curious pickle, I'm sorry to say. It appears, if you please, he may have got some girl pregnant."

"Indeed."

How very dryly that was spoken. He wondered if the word pregnant had been too indelicate. But what else could he have said? Every other term he knew was coarser.

"He actually wanted me to tell him if it would be morally wrong for him as a Christian to marry her without loving her."

"A pity he didn't apply his Christian scruples sooner."

"Good Lord, yes."

"Did he admit to being responsible?"

"Yes, he did; but in a curiously confused way."

"I'm sure. Did he say who she is?"

"You see, Elizabeth, I naturally assumed she must be one of those dubious ladies from Glasgow. But no, he says she's local."

"Did he mention her name?"

"Yes, he did. Agnes Tolmie, I think it was."

119

This time the pause was so long he wondered if they had been cut off. He sighed interrogatively.

"I'm still here. Disgusted and astounded. This is a bombshell."

"You're so right, Elizabeth. Who'd ever have thought it of Luke Dilworth?"

"Who'd ever have thought it of Agnes Tolmie."

"Why, do you know the girl, Elizabeth?"

"She worked in the hotel during the summer."

"Ah, so she's a maid?"

"She's a school-teacher."

"A school-teacher?"

"It was a summer job. Dilworth's been going about with her for some time."

"I didn't know that."

"I don't think he wanted people to know."

"She wouldn't be the girl who was with him and Miss Ann when the little dog was killed?"

"That was Agnes."

"I thought you mentioned she came from a very respectable family."

"I doubt if there's a girl in all Scotland who had a stricter upbringing. Her father's a lay preacher. They belong to a sect with extremely righteous views."

"I see. So this may be a case of extreme reaction against extreme repression?"

Elizabeth actually laughed. "I must admit I feel very disappointed. As you know I hold no brief for ridiculously narrow views, but there was a certain quaint interest in watching the experiment of a girl being brought up in our rather lax times as strictly as a girl might have been in John Knox's Scotland. I wondered how she would turn out. At school they thought her sly, but I was inclined to put that down to a defensiveness she probably found necessary. She went to college and became a teacher. She's teaching in Glen Canach."

"Trixie and I took the children a picnic there in summer. A beautiful tranquil spot."

"Her headmistress was, indeed still is for all I know, greatly impressed by her. Agnes was doing wonderfully well. Miss Breckinridge is no idle praiser. I thought: well, little Agnes seems to be doing what she was brought up to do."

"And what was that, Elizabeth?"

"I suppose to keep at bay all the trivialities and cheap temptations of our time."

"A noble but prodigious task."

"We all have our fancies, Harry. Now, alas, she's turned out to be cheap and trivial herself."

"Still, Elizabeth, as the poet said: to err is human, to forgive divine."

"It's not for me either to forgive or condemn her."

"I think it is, you know, Elizabeth. You feel let down. Will you be having a word with her?"

"Why on earth should I? She's got parents."

"But if they're so strict they may not be helpful in a crisis like this."

"She's got an uncle and aunt who are worldly enough."

He wondered if she saw the implication: so often Christians turned their backs and left the Lord's work to be done by infidels.

"I feel I have a responsibility towards Luke," he said. "After all, he did come to me for advice."

"So you said, Harry. The young fool's trying to wriggle out of it."

"Perhaps that's putting it rather harshly, Elizabeth. What you've told me about Miss Tolmie has interested me. You know, there could be another way altogether of looking at this romance."

"Romance?"

"Why not? Two religiously minded young people in love, too unworldly to take precautions."

"I thought he told you he wasn't in love?"

"Ah, that could have been his rather touching way of expressing his sense of unworthiness."

Her voice became as hard as Trixie's. "You do as you think best, Harry. I'm sorry for her father. I'm sorry for us all. I feel she's deceived and cheapened us. Good night."

"Good night, Elizabeth."

He put down the telephone. He would have liked to stay there and pray for guidance, but he thought it more prudent to go upstairs and at least offer assistance to Trixie if the children were proving tiresome.

5

NEXT MORNING WHEN he came to the road junction Mr Stiegel turned the blue nose of his little British Mini in the direction of Glen Canach, away from the *Perseus* and Ardhallow. After last night's rain and wind it was a cool clear sunny morning with birds singing. He sang too, cheerfully but not loudly enough to startle any passing motorist or stationary countryman. These, though, were rare, as the road and the whole countryside were empty of people.

Even if he had not started out with the feeling that his mission of reconciliation was sanctified he would surely have acquired it, in that vast beautiful wilderness of bare mountain, shining water, grey dykes, and solitary pines. Long before he came to the huge sequoias at the entrance to the glen he had begun, in a curious way that he had experienced before, to feel exalted and almost pure spirit, so that his hands on the steering wheel and the face he caught glimpses of in the rear mirror were strangers, in spite of the wedding ring given by Trixie and the dark glasses he always wore out of doors.

When he arrived at the school he drove straight into the playground, not knowing this was against Miss Breckinridge's regulations. Entering the small high-roofed building he knocked boldly on the first door he came to. Assiduous chanting of the eight times table was issuing from it. From the adjacent room came laughter and shouting, as if there discipline and diligence were not so good.

Miss Breckinridge, having silenced her chanters, opened the door. He did not know it but she had once heard him preach a sermon of embarrassing homeliness from St Aidan's dignified pulpit. Nor did he know that a ribbon round a wild squirrel's neck in her view would not have been less appropriate than the narrow trousers of shepherd's tartan and the checked lumberman's shirt were on him. Another thing he did not know was that Miss Breckinridge, though as patriotic as anyone else, was not satisfied in her conscience that H-bombs, those inventions of the devil, could morally be used by Christians, even as threats. She knew how many children had been killed at Hiroshima.

She had also been one of those affronted by the big Cross in lights shining above the *Perseus* at Christmas.

Luckily he was not aware of all this. He thought her sternness a consequence of her job.

"Sorry to interrupt your good work, madam," he said, enthusiastically. "Allow me to introduce myself."

"I know who you are, Mr Stiegel."

He was delighted. "Excellent. I've come to see Miss Tolmie who, I believe, teaches school here."

"She does."

"In there?" He jerked his thumb in the direction of the laughter and shouting. "They seem to be having a real good time in there."

"Which does not mean they are not learning."

He was not aware of the magnanimity of that admission. Miss Breckinridge's own class remained silent: that was how she had trained them. But she was more and more prepared to believe that learning could be a noisy happy process, even if it meant questioning her own practice over thirty years.

"On the contrary, madam," he cried. "Happy children are good children, and good children are learning children."

That was the sort of gush she could never stand.

"I hope your business with Miss Tolmie is important," she said stiffly. "I don't like lessons being interrupted."

"I promise not to keep her away from her valuable work more than a couple of minutes."

"I hope it's not about her mother."

"No. Is her mother ill then?"

"In hospital, about to undergo a serious operation."

"Yet Miss Tolmie carries on, so courageously!"

"She has her work to do."

The headmistress opened Agnes's door. Peals of merriment came out. "Agnes," she called. "Someone to see you." Then she went back into her own room where within seconds the purposeful chanting began again.

Mr Stiegel hardly heard it. The small girl who now stood before him was not, as the Scotch said, bonny. But it was no disadvantage; on the contrary, it seemed to him to let another much rarer quality, spiritual sureness, shine through. Had she been beautiful he would have suspected falseness somewhere.

These were eyes of a truly devout honesty. Yet they were far from solemn: they sparkled with the kind of happiness that came from having looked upon the promised land; part of which was assuredly her love for Luke and his for her.

Mr Stiegel felt humbly grateful that it had fallen to him to reconcile so rare a pair of lovers.

He held out his hand. "I'm Harry Stiegel, Miss Tolmie."

"Yes, I know. I've seen you before, and of course Luke's told me a lot about you."

"I'm here, in a way, on Luke's behalf."

She laughed. "If he's sent you to say you'll marry us,

Mr Stiegel, I'm sorry. It's already been arranged. We're going to be married in St Aidan's, by Mr Plenderleith. I hope Dora will be my maid of honour, and Ann my bridesmaid if she's well enough."

Mr Stiegel wondered why Luke, shy fellow, had kept this good news dark.

"I didn't know the arrangements were so far forward," he said.

The door opened and a small boy, with the reddest hair and the most mischievous eyes Mr Stiegel had ever seen, peeped out and asked: "Is it all right if I put the red paint on now, Miss Tolmie?"

"Yes, Hamish. But put it on the fort and not on yourself, or anybody else."

"I promise." He went back in again, with astonishing eagerness.

"It's history," said Miss Tolmie. "They've made a fort. There's been a battle. Hamish asked to do the blood. He'll make an awful mess."

Mr Stiegel hoped that Harry Junior one day was lucky enough to get a teacher as understanding as Miss Tolmie.

"Pardon my frankness," he whispered, with a smile. "I assure you I am a well-wisher. I understand you are expecting a child?"

"Yes."

Elizabeth Greenloaning would have looked for shame in those shining eyes. Harry Stiegel looked for reverence for life, and found it almost to excess. This girl would never allow a contraceptive device near her. She would scorn the first whisper of abortion.

"And of course Luke is the father?"

She was silent for almost a quarter of a minute; then with a burst of her merriest laughter she cried: "Would it really matter?"

He had to laugh too, in excitement, though he felt confused.

"We are all God's children," she said.

"Very true."

"Without Him there could be no children, could there? They can't make babies in test tubes, can they?"

"Indeed they cannot."

"All those trees out there, they're the Lord's too, aren't they? And all the salmon in the river. It doesn't really matter who their fathers are, does it? The Lord's everybody's and everything's father, isn't He?"

Mr Stiegel was overwhelmed by those ecstatic, slightly hysterical, terribly sure questions. Of course they made sense, too glorious for everyday use. The Forestry Commission no doubt would allow the Lord ownership of the trees, for there was no chance of His cutting them down and selling them. And the landlords who owned the fishing rights would raise no objection if the Lord's mystical rod caught the entire complement of salmon. Even in human terms no father would ever deny the Lord a role in the conception of his children. Otherwise where would those children get souls? No man had any need to be jealous of the Lord.

It had not been by intellectual effort, as in the case of professional theologians, that this remarkable young woman had arrived at the profoundly Christian conclusion, that all living things, trees, fish, and people, had in them the essence of the Lord. She knew it through a simplicity and yet a profundity of faith such as Mr Stiegel had never before encountered.

The door of Miss Breckinridge's room opened and she looked out. It was really to see if he had taken off those ridiculous sun-glasses. He hadn't, so she said, sharply: "Agnes, your children are much too noisy." Then she withdrew.

It was a hint to Mr Stiegel. He took it gratefully: best go while faith was still singing hosannas in his soul.

Shaking hands again with Miss Tolmie and whispering

that he would surely speak with her again, he took his leave, and was in his car, manoeuvring round a great tree stump in the playground, before he remembered that he had not got after all a definite assurance that Luke really was the father of the child. But to suspect Miss Tolmie of having artfully dodged the question would have been like accusing Christ of temporising with the Pharisees.

About an hour later he was himself finding the telling of the truth difficult. This wasn't because he wanted to hide or distort anything, or because he could not see what the truth was: it was because of the obduracy of the person to whom he was trying to tell it.

Returning from Glen Canach he went straight to his small office in the navy complex on shore. There he at once rang up Elizabeth Greenloaning. He had to tell someone about this discovery he had made, and Elizabeth was a more suitable confidante than Trixie.

Alas, he had meant her to admire and rejoice at the gem of spirituality he had unearthed, not, rather testily and too readily, to doubt its genuineness.

"What on earth are you talking about, Harry?" she asked, interrupting his gush of words. "Have you seen Agnes then?"

"Yes, I have been to Glen Canach, and I must say I was tremendously impressed."

"Yes, it is a beautiful spot. Too many midges, though."

"It was Miss Tolmie I was tremendously impressed by."

"Indeed."

"I think I could say that I have seldom met anyone in whom the Lord was more fruitfully at work."

"Are you referring to her pregnancy?"

He suspected sarcasm. "I am referring to the joy of the Lord that shines in her eyes."

"Just one moment, Harry. You aren't speaking of some saint you've discovered in a convent on a high mountain;

127

you're speaking of Agnes Tolmie whom I've known for years. Heaven knows I don't want to disparage her, but I must ask you, please, not to provoke me. Really, Harry, Trixie's right, you know: you do exaggerate."

She laughed, but it was steely laughter that reinforced her rebuke.

"You're not the first Agnes has taken in," she added.

"I was not taken in. She made absolutely no attempt to take me in. She was transparently frank, and infectiously happy. I tell you, Elizabeth, everything I saw on my way home, trees, stones, people, had in them a deeper reality because of Miss Tolmie."

"What on earth is a deeper reality?" she asked, quite snappishly.

He began to understand why Mr Oliphant, a man of influence in the community, deferred to her; he had once remarked that the man wasn't born who could get the better of Miss Greenloaning in business. Mr Stiegel at the time, with a manly whisky in his hand and one in his stomach, had accepted the remark as praise. Now he saw that he, a minister of God, ought to have higher standards than a lawyer who paid too much homage to power and money.

"There is a round pebble on my desk, Elizabeth," he said, dramatically.

"Yes?"

"I picked it up years ago on an Oregon beach, when I was on my honeymoon. It is dark blue, with irregular pink whirls through it. I do not know its geological name. It is very smooth, from the washing of a million tides."

"Yes?"

"Most of the time it just lies here and is simply a pretty stone, useful as a paperweight. But sometimes as I look at it, as I had it in my hand, I feel that it, and my own soul, are fresh from the crucible of God. Do you follow me, Elizabeth?"

"Easily, Harry. Any Christian would. Surely we all have such feelings?"

Envying her that depth and plenitude of faith he at the same time doubted her right to have it. She was after all an untested Christian. Never in her life had she suffered materially or spiritually. She had had to traverse no deserts. Surrounded always by as much comfort as she wished, and by friends who had caused her no grief or anger, she had never really been given a chance to find out how the faith she so confidently claimed would stand up to a confrontation with evil. Probably she would try to explain evil away in terms of unfortunate heredity and bad social conditions.

"You haven't said yet if she admitted to being pregnant."

"She didn't merely admit it, Elizabeth, she gloried in it. And why not? Is not every child that's conceived a part of God?"

"Ideally, yes. But hardly in practice, Harry. Too many children are born in squalor, brutality, and degrading poverty."

"Even so they are part of God. It is the foundation of our faith. We undermine it at our peril. Miss Tolmie believes it as naturally as she breathes."

"Is she thinking of getting married?"

"Robert could answer that better than I."

"What do you mean?"

"They are to be married by him, in his church, with Dora and Ann as bridesmaids."

She gasped. "Did she tell you that?"

"She did, proudly."

A long pause, "I can't think what her reason could be, It's not true. She's never spoken to Robert about any such thing. In any case, neither she nor her parents have ever been members of St Aidan's."

"Does that matter, Elizabeth? In Christ's eyes surely all His churches are one?"

"That may be so, Harry, but we all have our rules and find it convenient to abide by them. Good night."

He found himself with a dead telephone in his hand and horror flickering in his heart. Were atheists who declared Christianity the most monstrous hoax in history going to be proved right, not by ministers as often in deserts of doubt as in oases of certainty, but by adherents like Miss Greenloaning, impeccably respectable, flawlessly charitable, and resolutely fair-minded, but devoid of passion and wonder?

6

ONE EVENING ABOUT a week after his visit to the chaplain's house Luke was crouched in the launch crossing from the *Perseus* to the jetty, at the end of the day's work. It was cold and wet, as it had been all day, and the day before. The men were all huddled into their short thick coats, silent and subdued, as if they too had problems crushing them. Blasphemous complaints about the weather were puffed out with cigarette smoke; similarly blasphemous thanks that the speaker's stint of duty in this rainy God-forsaken hole would soon be over and he'd get back to sunny California. None was in a mood to talk intimately, to get close to anyone else. This early darkness, this rain and cold, repeated from yesterday and probably to be repeated again tomorrow, and so on through a long winter, were forcing every man in upon himself.

As he was climbing out on to the slippery jetty Luke stumbled. He was steadied by the sailor behind him. This was a strong big-nosed low-browed man called Chuck Nelson. On previous occasions he had given Luke some winks and nudges. Luke knew of him as a foul-mouthed good-natured man who frequented bars and whores.

They walked together along the jetty towards the waiting taxis.

"You Luke Dilworth?" asked Nelson, in a friendly voice.

"Yes."

"Well, how are things?"

"Fine."

"Sure?"

"Yes."

"No troubles?"

"No."

"Well, that's dandy. Fucking awful weather this. Still, should wash the dog-shit off the sidewalks."

With a cheerful tap on Luke's shoulder he went off laughing, like a man relieved.

Luke felt his own heart lightened. If kindness towards a stranger was in a man like Nelson, it must be in everyone. The world was better than he had been giving it credit for.

Agnes's uncle was there with his taxi. He and Luke always avoided each other.

Luke shared with three older men. One was black. They were patiently eager to get to their families across in Greenock. They chatted about their children happy at their Scottish school.

As he listened Luke tried again to see Agnes as his wife. Mr Stiegel, seeking him out on the ship, had said he had never met a young woman in whom the joy of the Lord was so strong. Certainly she was happy in a way hard otherwise to explain, for her mother was in hospital and her father had disowned her. Luke had sometimes wondered, after the episode in the bedroom, whether she was quite sane, or at any rate normal; but, though Mr Stiegel was laughed at by the men because of his exaggerations, still he was a cleverer man than Luke, with more experience, and his reason for Agnes's buoyancy was more likely to be true.

Last Sunday when he had taken her back to Glen Canach she had introduced him to her landlady. Mrs McTeague had praised her sincerely.

Nor was she as unattractive as he had at first thought. Granny had said she was a flower that had got too little sun; now that she was getting her fair share, she was blooming.

Her breasts had surprised him. They had been beautiful. Thinking of them could make desire stir in him.

The taxi stopped at the pier. He got off too, though it was ten minutes' walk from there to Granny's; and it was still raining.

One of the men patted him on the back. "Cheer up, boy," he said. "They say the sun shines again come May."

"I don't mind the rain," replied Luke, eagerly.

They went into the pier laughing at his brave little joke.

Coat collar pulled up, and hands thrust into pockets, he walked slowly by way of the West Bay, a crescent of pebbly shore, with gardens as long as football fields running up to the big hotels, all closed for the winter. Lamplight gleamed bluely on the pebbles that the waves pushed out and sucked back in again with a continuous roar. In the dark sea flashed the two lighthouses that guarded the entrance to the firth, or, as he saw it, the exit, for beyond those steadfast flashes, across the dark Atlantic, lay home.

Again he thought of Agnes. He remembered her sensible conduct on the day the dog was killed. All his life he would remember Ann Plenderleith, but he knew he would never have married her, even if her father and Miss Greenloaning had approved of him. Every time he compared Agnes with Ann he found to his surprise that he had more in common with the former.

As he pushed open the gate he thought of Agnes's mother very ill after her operation. During the past two weeks he had often caught sight of poor Mr Tolmie gazing at him, as if minded to come and make peace.

There must be a comic programme on the television. Standing on the doorstep, he could hear the brays of laughter from the studio audience. He couldn't, though, hear Granny's own yelps of enjoyment. He smiled. She must be in one of her disdainful moods when she would watch grimly and refuse to laugh at "sich eedjits, paid a hundred times mair than the dustman, and no' half as useful".

He opened the door. Out streaked Mick the cat, past him and round the corner. As Granny said, cats, like folk, did daft things when they got old.

He took off his wet coat and hat and hung them on the stand, beside the brass plaque embossed with thistles.

"It's me, Granny," he called. "It's sure some place for rain, your Ardhallow."

A burst of laughter answered him. When you weren't watching the screen sure enough this laughter did sound idiotic. He smiled at the old woman's shrewdness.

On his way to wash he opened the living-room door. With a chuckle he saw that Granny had fallen asleep, with her look of scorn. The two comedians strutted and wise-cracked in vain. Tiptoeing in, he turned the volume down. He half expected Granny to wake up and order him to turn it up again: they might be "eedjits", but they were company. But no, she was too sound asleep.

He ate in the kitchen. Mick came scratching and miaowing at the back door, but refused to come in when Luke opened it. Tail stiff, the old cat miaowed fiercely. He thought he heard Granny shout to shut the door, there was a draught.

He went to the living-room to tell her about Mick. But she was still asleep. It couldn't have been her who'd

133

called. He stood smiling at her, and the two pink-and-gold china dogs smiled back. Between them Mr Brisbane in the faded photograph tried to smile too.

Suddenly something about her, perhaps the way her shiny withered hand dangled, alarmed him. He put his hand, very tenderly, on her brow.

"Granny, wake up," he kept whispering, though he knew it was useless, she was dead. That was why poor old Mick couldn't bear to stay in the house.

He crouched and pressed her hand against his face. He wept, not just because an old woman who had been kind to him was dead, but also because with her death, with her quietly leaving him at this difficult time, he felt more alone than ever before and did not know what to do.

A few minutes later, in a panic, he realised he ought to have summoned a doctor or the police. So he put on his coat and hat and ran out into the pouring rain, along the street towards the telephone box.

He asked the operator to put him through to the police.

A slow cautious cheerful very Scotch voice spoke: "Ardhallow Police Station, Sergeant Brownlie speaking."

"Name's Dilworth, sir, Luke Dilworth of the U.S.S. *Perseus*. I live with old Mrs Brisbane, in Bullwood Road."

"Take your time, lad. Old Granny, do you mean?"

"That's right, sir. She's dead. I came home and found her dead in her chair. I thought she was just asleep."

"I see. Well, take it easy, lad. She was very old. This was to be expected. She went peacefully."

"She must have been watching the television. It was still on."

"Do you happen to ken who her doctor was?"

"Dr Milne, I think. He's old too."

"But still more than fit for his job. He'll no' thank us for getting him oot on a night like this. I'll drop in myself for a minute. I'd like to see everything's all right for the old lady."

"Thank you, sir."

"You were fond of her?"

"Yes, sir."

"By the way, Dilworth you said?"

"That's right."

"I've heard your name this night already. I understand you are acquainted with a boy called Tommy Springburn. He lives at the Home. Mrs Maxwell mentioned you among his acquaintances: a very short list, I may say."

"I haven't seen little Tommy for weeks. Is there anything wrong?"

"No, no. It's just that he's forgotten to return after school today."

"But school finishes at four!"

"Well, it's not long past six now. You ken what boys are. They forget when to return. I expect he's stravaiging aboot, hands in pockets, whistling his head off, without a care in the world."

The rain beat against the kiosk.

"On a night like this, sir?"

"Well maybe it's not the best of nights to be stravaiging the streets. He'll be in somebody's house."

"I don't think he knows anybody, sir. Is there a search party out? I'd like to help."

"Wait now, we're still hoping he'll turn up, soaked but cheery. There's a police car roaming the streets on the look-out."

"Miss Ann Plenderleith, the minister's daughter, knows him best."

"Mrs Maxwell mentioned another girl, one you're acquainted with."

"Miss Tolmie?"

"Aye, that's her. According to Mrs Maxwell she's the only one he's taken to."

Last Sunday in the taxi Agnes had talked about taking the boy to live with them once they were married. Luke hadn't taken her seriously.

"Maybe he's gone to her," suggested the sergeant.

"But she's at Glen Canach, twenty miles away."

"He could have got a lift. We're trying to get in touch with her, to warn her he might turn up. In the meantime, lad, keep your eyes open."

"Yes, sir."

As he walked back to the house, shivering, he tried to imagine himself in the boy's place. In the whole world there wasn't a single human being who admitted to any responsibility for you other than legal. If you didn't come back, if your body was found on the pebbles or floating under the pier, the tears that might be shed would not be the spontaneous, marvellous and consoling tears of instinctive love, but only the tears of pity and honourable duty. Even as he respected the care and kindness of Mrs Maxwell and her helpers, he remembered his own mother's love for him which nothing could weaken. If he were to become a criminal, a murderer even, hounded by the whole community, she would still love him and try to protect him.

When Tommy had come out of school at four, other children would have been shouting and playing around him. He had paid them no heed. He had walked to no shop or house. He was still walking, in this rain; or perhaps by this time, tired and hungry, he had lain down behind some wall, waiting, like an animal, for whatever might happen.

But perhaps the truth was less tragic. Perhaps he was hiding somewhere in the Home grounds. In the morning he would wake up stiff, cold, hungry, but glad, and he would go into the house where he would be scolded, anxiously but fondly, given a hot bath, and put to bed.

Luke lingered at the gate. Mick came and rubbed

136

against his legs. The Tolmies' house was in darkness. Mr Tolmie would be visiting his wife in hospital.

A police car came splashing along the road. A white-haired sergeant got out, followed by the driver, a policeman as young as Luke.

"Constable Hislop," said the sergeant. "I'm Sergeant Brownlie. You'll be Mr Dilworth?"

"Yes, sir."

"Doctor not here yet?"

"No, sir."

"No sign of the boy?"

"No, sir."

The rain drummed on the policemen's hard hats.

"If I was going to run away," said Hislop, "by Christ I'd pick a better night than this."

"And you'd make sure you had a place to run to," said the sergeant.

"Must be weak in the head."

"Well, here's the doctor. He was at the hospital."

The doctor, hat on carelessly, was as lively in mind as he was shaky in the legs.

"Hello, Sergeant. Scene of the crime, eh? This the young fellow who found her? Well, let's get out of this damn rain; it's bad for my rheumatics."

Luke opened the door for him.

"Many a time I've been in this house," he said, as he went in. "I liked to look in and have a crack."

He went into the living-room. "So you were as good as your word, Nellie," he said. "You said you'd die with your fingers at your nose, and you damned nearly have."

He examined her. "Well, you're dead enough, Nellie. Nothing for me to do. Or Plenderleith or Shearer or any of our gentlemen of the cloth. Only Willie Liddlestane's got work here. The town undertaker," he explained to Luke.

"Shouldn't she be put to bed, sir?" asked Luke.

"You think she'll be more comfortable there? Right. Constable, you're a fine beefy fellow, lend a hand."

"Let me, sir," said Luke.

So it was he, holding her shoulders, and Hislop holding her feet, who carried Granny into her room and laid her on the bed.

The doctor covered her with a sheet. "Well, you'll have company, Nellie," he said. "Her neighbour, Mrs Tolmie, died a couple of hours ago, in the hospital. A patient of mine. I thought we'd saved her. But no."

"Will Tolmie's wife?" asked the sergeant.

"Aye. Said his prayers were better than any surgeon's knife. I don't know what he's saying now, on his knees, at her bedside. I know what night sister's saying; that she wishes he'd go."

"A man that believes as deeply as him," said the sergeant cannily, "can't see daith as the end surely. He's bound to think she's in a better place already."

"Or a worse," said the doctor cheerfully. "Well, I'm for off. I could do with a dram. You look as if you could too," he added to Luke. "Would you like me to drop you outside a pub?"

Luke was anxious about Agnes. "Was Mrs Tolmie's daughter at the hospital, sir?"

"Wee Agnes? No, she hadn't arrived. Her uncle was sent to bring her in his taxi. Wouldn't put it past him charging her a fare. You know Agnes?"

"She lived next door."

"So she did. Strange child. Once had to put a dozen stitches in her backside; she'd fallen on glass. Didn't utter a cheep. The Lord, said her father, was watching. So He was, judging from her eyes. Well, good night, all."

They watched him run through the rain to his car and drive away.

"What about you?" asked the sergeant. "You're not too scared to stay the night?"

"No, sir."

"Well, if you change your mind and want to find a place, give me a ring."

"Thank you, sir. I'll do that."

He watched them hurry to their car and drive away.

7

HE COULD NOT settle, even to read the Bible. He went out into the garden with a plateful of cat's meat and called to Mick. The cat would be company. But it did not come.

The Tolmies' house was still dark. He wondered what Mr Tolmie could have prayed for, at his dead wife's bedside. It seemed to him that any request or wish or demand on behalf of the dead must be an impertinence on the part of the living. Freed from all bodily needs and weaknesses, and from fear, greed, and desire, surely the dead were already in a state of happiness and freedom that could not be improved.

In the rain-shrouded firth a ship sounded its siren. The sudden hoarse loud noise startled him; he imagined it came out of the sky and was rebuking him...

He decided he would go out, to look for Tommy, or meet Agnes at the hospital, or visit the Plenderleiths, or go to a pub, or just walk in the rain.

The streets were empty. All Ardhallow was at home, watching television by the fire. Even the main street was deserted. Men who liked to go singing from one pub to another, for a change of jollity, stayed put tonight.

He stared into every doorway. On the sea front, where the waves splashed up, he searched all the shelters and peered down at the rocks that glittered in the lamplight.

Coming to a telephone box he went in, not sure whom he wanted to ring, Mr Plenderleith or Mr Stiegel or Agnes at the hospital or Mrs Maxwell at the Home.

He chose Mrs Maxwell.

"Kilbridge Home, Matron Maxwell speaking," said a woman, tired but eager.

"Good evening, ma'm. Sorry to bother you. I'd like to know if young Tommy's come back yet."

"No, he hasn't. Who are you? What do you know about it?"

"My name's Dilworth, ma'm. Sergeant Brownlie told me."

"You're Agnes Tolmie's friend, aren't you?"

"Yes, ma'm."

"Do you think he's trying to go to her?"

"I don't think he'd know the way. In any case, ma'm, Agnes is in town. At the hospital. You see, her mother died there this evening."

"Who told you that?"

"Dr Milne."

"I don't suppose Tommy could be at the hospital, with Agnes?"

"I wouldn't think so, ma'm."

"I'll phone anyway. Where are you phoning from?"

"Down by the sea. I've been looking."

"What's the use on a night like this? I don't know what I could have done. I tried everything."

"Yes, ma'm. I'm sure he'll turn up. Good night."

Outside in the rain again he stood hesitating: should he go now to the hospital and see Agnes? But when he started walking it was in the direction of Mr Plenderleith's manse. All the way there he could find no reason for going, and when he was ringing the door bell he still had found none.

It was Dora who opened the door. She was wearing spectacles and had a book in her hand. At first she didn't recognise him.

"Good evening, Miss Dora," he said. "It's me, Luke Dilworth."

"Goodness, so it is. You're soaked. Have you come to see my father? You'd better come in."

Taking off his cap, he stepped into the hall. There were golf clubs in the corner.

She smiled at him in peculiar amusement. "I believe we've been expecting you," she said.

"Because of Tommy, you mean?"

She frowned. "No. Don't mention him, please. We don't want Ann to know."

"He's still lost."

"I doubt if he's lost. Elizabeth's right: this is his way of attracting attention."

He thought that no one in the world had wanted attention less.

She smiled again. "Because of what Agnes told Mr Stiegel."

He didn't understand.

"About getting my father to marry you in St Aidan's."

Her father came out of the sitting-room. He was wearing green slippers.

"Thought I recognised your voice, Luke," he said.

"He's awfully embarrassed," said Dora, laughing. "Well, I'll leave you to discuss it."

She went into the sitting-room. Luke heard Miss Greenloaning say something to her.

Mr Plenderleith put his hand on Luke's arm. He lowered his voice.

"So you and Agnes are to be married soon?" he said.

"Yes, sir."

"I suppose, in her happiness, Agnes has gone on with the arrangements without consulting anyone. However, I shall be pleased to do the trick. All three of us will have to have a meeting soon. Now you'd best come in to the fire. Did Dora say anything to you about the boy?"

"Yes, sir."

"Apparently he's run off. We had a call from Mrs Maxwell. We think it better if Ann doesn't know. She's almost recovered, thank God, but unpleasant or distressing subjects must be kept from her."

"I understand, sir."

"Good."

They went into the sitting-room. Looking for Ann Luke didn't see her immediately. Miss Greenloaning sat in an armchair by the fire, Dora in another.

Then he saw Ann. Half hidden by the curtains, she was looking out of the window, The *Perseus* was down there, all lit up; its dynamoes could be heard humming. Was it no longer considered an unpleasant or distressing subject?

"Good evening, Luke," said Miss Greenloaning, curtly affable. "Is it still raining as heavily as ever?"

"Pouring," said Dora.

"You're soaked," said Miss Greenloaning. "Shouldn't you take that coat off?" But she suggested it in such a way that he thought she didn't really expect him to do it.

Slowly Ann came over. She wore a thick white jumper and looked fat. He sensed the others turning a little stiff; they glanced at one another, and at him, like plotters afraid lest this stranger in their midst might learn something he ought not to.

Ann was changed. Her face was fat, her eyes dull; she breathed loudly. He wondered if she had been under treatment by drugs. He thought of Agnes whose drug, if it could be called that, was belief in God, or rather, for it wasn't quite the same thing, her certainty that whatever happened to her, whatever she did, God would support her. He had seen her unhappy but never defeated. Ann looked as if she had given in. He remembered the high standards she had set herself and other people. Apparently she had been persuaded those were not possible, and was now content with the same standards as everybody else.

"Hello," she said.

"Hello."

He waited, but she seemed quite satisfied with the long silence.

"Luke was just passing, my dear," said her father. "Very thoughtfully he dropped in to see how you were. How we all were," he added quickly, at a signal from Miss Greenloaning. "Please sit down, Ann. Otherwise poor Luke will have to keep standing too, I see."

Luke was uncomfortably aware his coat was beginning to steam and smell. Miss Greenloaning's nose twitched, and the small smile of reassurance she gave him was even more disturbing.

Their restraint and their different kind of politeness made them as alien as if they had been Chinese. He could not tell what they were thinking or feeling. Even if Ann had not been there making them cautious they would still have preferred him not to mention Tommy or Granny or Mrs Tolmie. They would not be comfortable if a stranger like him came into their house and began to speak about subjects that they would have had to respond to deeply. They weren't ever entirely honest with themselves; as he realised that, he wondered if anyone ever was or could be.

"I hear you're going to marry Agnes Tolmie," said Ann.

The others looked uncomfortable.

"Yes," he said.

"I haven't seen Agnes for weeks," said Dora. "I hear she's very happy at Glen Canach."

"I don't want to see her," remarked Ann.

The very casualness of the remark seemed to chill them. Mr Plenderleith sighed, Dora gave a little shudder, and Miss Greenloaning frowned.

"I've never liked her," added Ann, just as casually.

"All your people at home keeping well, I hope, Luke?" asked Mr Plenderleith.

"Yes sir, thank you."

"And your old landlady, is she keeping well?"

Luke hesitated. "Yes, sir." His voice trembled.

"Is her house still as smelly?" asked Ann.

It was Miss Greenloaning's turn to man the breach. "Ann, my dear," she murmured, "she's a very old woman. Not so easy for her to keep her house clean."

"She wouldn't take a home help. I tried to get her to. She preferred to be dirty."

"Perhaps she preferred to be independent," suggested Mr Plenderleith.

"I don't know why you're defending her, Elizabeth," said Ann. "You'd have been horrified. You used to think Torch was smelly."

It was now Dora's turn. "How is Agnes's mother?" she asked. "I heard she's had an operation and is going to be all right."

Luke nodded.

"When I was in hospital yesterday," said Mr Plenderleith, "visiting two of my parishioners, I had a word with Mrs Tolmie. She seemed tired and confused, poor woman, but they seemed to think she had a good chance of recovery."

When they learned that Granny and Mrs Tolmie were dead they would blame him for deceiving them. You didn't have to say it, they would say, you could have told us in some other way that Ann wouldn't have noticed. You have made us look foolish and heartless.

Miserably he wondered, as he sat among them, what that other way could be.

Suddenly Miss Greenloaning put down her magazine and got to her feet.

"Well, Robert," she said, "I must be going. If you like, Luke, I could drop you off at Granny's gate. It's not far out of my way."

"Why are you taking him away?" asked Ann. "He's not saying anything he shouldn't."

"Nobody's taking him away, Ann," said Miss Greenloaning with a smile. "I merely offered him a lift. It's a very wet night, you know."

Luke had hurriedly stood up. "Thank you, Miss Greenloaning," he said.

"Will you be taking Agnes to America with you?" asked Ann.

"I expect so."

"You don't sound very enthusiastic." She came close to him. "Do you see Tommy often?" she asked.

"No. I haven't seen him for some time."

She stared at him for almost half a minute, while the others waited anxiously.

"It doesn't matter, does it?" she said, and went over to the window again.

Mr Plenderleith accompanied his fiancée and Luke into the hall. He took from a bag of golf clubs a large multi-coloured umbrella.

"I hope the lad is found soon," he said. "For his own sake, of course. But for Ann's too."

"Yes," murmured Miss Greenloaning, "we must hope that. But even if the worst was to happen and he never was found—"

"God forbid, Elizabeth!"

"—I don't think it would cause a relapse. She's learned to give things their real value. That's a lesson never forgotten."

Mr Plenderleith sighed. "What would be the real value of a child's disappearance, my dear? If it were permanent?"

She smiled at him with love but also with reproof. He ought not to have asked such a question.

She opened the door and stepped out into the rain. The minister followed quickly and put up the big umbrella.

All three huddled under it as they went down the steps to the car.

"Don't look so worried, Robert," she said, as she got ready to start the engine. "I expect he's safe in bed by this time, after a hot supper."

She smiled, patted his hand, and then switched on the engine. She drove off quickly without a glance back. She was no longer smiling.

They were driving along the sea-front before she spoke. Her voice was cold.

"I may say Mr Stiegel told us more than that you and Agnes were to be married."

He could think of nothing to say.

"Hardly in confidence," she went on. "That kind of information can only be concealed for a short time. Is it true?"

He wasn't quite sure what she meant.

"Is Agnes pregnant?"

He nodded. "She says so."

"Of course you'd just have to take her word for it. But you must know if it could be true."

Again he nodded.

"What does that mean? It could be true? Very well."

She was silent for a few seconds, during which he thought that, though she was rich and good-looking and highly respected, she was more predictable and limited than Agnes. She had shrugged her shoulders at Tommy run away, Agnes had plans to adopt him.

"If she is pregnant," went on Miss Greenloaning, "then it's out of the question for her to be married in St Aidan's. Robert, Mr Plenderleith, will marry you, but not in the church. At Agnes's house, in my hotel if she wishes."

"It doesn't matter," he murmured.

"It does to me. A church is a sacred place; it ought not to be mocked. Not all of us make a public display of our faith. I happen to believe that a woman who has got herself pregnant before marriage has forfeited her right to be married in a church."

He was astonished by her passion. She was not so predictable after all. Agnes had once told him that the two women with whom she'd worked in the hotel had made jokes about Miss Greenloaning's very frequent visits to the manse. Could it be true that Miss Greenloaning had been tempted to do what could have made her pregnant? Or had she actually done it? When she said that Agnes had no right to be married in a church was she really accusing herself? It sounded like it. Otherwise why was she so distressed?

The car stopped by Granny's gate.

"Please tell Agnes," she said, "that I'm prepared, at my own expense, to provide a reception in the hotel."

"I'll tell her."

"Thank you."

He got out. They stared at each other.

"If I was you," she said, "I'd go straight in and get those wet clothes off."

He wondered if he should tell her now that Granny was dead in the house, and Agnes's mother dead in the hospital. He decided not to: she was one of those whose sympathy never worked though they said all the right words. She hadn't the gift of thinking only of others. Her own self was always present, however well-bred and discreet.

"Good night," she said, and drove away.

He waited at the gate only for a minute or so; then he set off towards the hospital. If he hurried he might be in time to catch Agnes there, and try to comfort her.

It took him twenty minutes. All lit up the hospital looked strangely cheerful, though he knew Agnes's mother lay dead in it and other people were probably dying or in pain. It wasn't only its lights that gave it its cheerful appearance; it was because after all the loneliness of that dark wet night, after seeing Granny dead and looking for Tommy and speaking to the Plenderleiths, he felt glad that he was going to meet Agnes. He felt suddenly dependent on her. She would comfort him more than he would her. As Mr Stiegel said she had a source of strength and happiness. All her life people had laughed at her, yet she had not grown bitter and revengeful. She had always been sure that one day her turn for happiness would come. The triumph would not be hers but the Lord's; it would be shown through her, that was all.

He felt pity for her, not derision, that at the very beginning of her triumph should come her father's disowning of her and now her mother's death. But she would still be triumphant.

He went through the glass doors into the empty reception hall.

"Visiting hour ended half an hour ago," called a woman from the office. She thought him drunk, because of his uniform and because his sodden trousers made him walk awkwardly.

He approached her, cap in hand. "I'm looking for Miss Tolmie," he said, "Miss Agnes Tolmie. Her mother died here this evening."

"Yes." Her tone was immediately contrite and sympathetic. "Are you a friend of hers?"

"Yes. I thought I might see her here."

"She left about half an hour ago, with her uncle and aunt."

She did not add, because she did not know how close to the Tolmies he was, and because in her job she had to be discreet, that Mr Tolmie, Agnes's father, had left the moment his daughter arrived, without saying a single word to her. All the night staff, and those patients who'd heard, were talking about it.

"Thank you," said Luke.

He would have liked to rest for a little while on one of the seats in the big quiet hall, but he could not, he had no reason to in the eyes of this watchful but pleasant woman, he would be as much out of place as he had been in Mr Plenderleith's manse or in Miss Greenloaning's car. He would have to find somewhere where he would not be out of place, where he would be at home.

Out in the rain again he walked on, thinking of places to go to. There was the club where he would find other American sailors, some of them perhaps as lonely as he. There was the taxi-driver's house, where he would find Agnes. Or he could take the old doctor's advice and go to a pub where for the price of a few whiskies he could buy forgetfulness.

In the main street he waited outside the biggest of the pubs. A man came out, and for the second that the door was opened laughter was heard, the laughter of men to whom the burden of life was as light as a glass of whisky.

He went in, and was amazed. He thought, so incongruously, of a church. It was spacious, with three pillars, so that though there were a number of men, some in American uniforms, they did not seem many, in groups at the bar, in alcoves, and round pillars. The bar gleamed like an altar, with bottles of various shapes and colours arrayed behind it. The two barkeeps, with towels over their shoulders, looked as solemn and dexterous as priests. But what most reinforced this church-like appearance, and saved it from blasphemy, was the attitude of the men. They laughed, they held glasses, they drank, but all the time they were serious in a peculiar masculine way that reminded him of other men praying.

While he was hesitating, not knowing what to do, like a newcomer in a synagogue or mosque, he was hailed from one of the alcoves by a sailor he knew slightly.

"Hey you, Dilworth, for Christ's sake."

At the same time he was approached by a small Scotsman with a red greedy face.

"Christ, Yank," he whispered, "you're as droont as a
herring. But here's Rab Gilliespie wanting to shake
your hand and welcome you to this corner of bonny
Scotland."

Luke had to suffer his hand being grabbed by one that,
podgy and busy, tried to convey half a dozen messages.

"Like to stand me a drink?" whispered the Scotsman.
"Care for a woman?"

Burroughs, the sailor who'd called to him, came over.

"Shocked to the balls to see a fellow like you in a sinful
place like this, Dilworth. Must be the weather. I was telling Stevie that the reason why the Scots are the second
worst alcoholics in Europe—that's true, you know, the
Irish are the worst—is because the only thing to do in a
fucking climate like theirs is to get drunk and forget it.
What's your poison, Dilworth? Scotch? The cleanest drink
in the world, the Scotch'll tell you. Every other drink,
gin, brandy, vodka, you name it, rots your gut; but not
Scotch, oh no, sir, it leaves your gut clean and fresh and
ready for more."

"'S true," muttered the Scotsman. "'S analysed and
proved."

"One thing it's good for," admitted Burroughs, "is for
warming you up when you're cold and wet. A double
Scotch for my friend," he called to the barkeep.

"You've got twa friends," mumbled the Scotsman.

"You fuck off, Jock," said Burroughs.

It was a foul word, and it was meant to convey an un-
kindness, yet he was able to say it cheerfully, with a manly
smile.

"Watch out for this little red-faced guy," he said. "He's
the worst scrounger in the town. The Scotch give him a
miss like leprosy."

The Scotsman did not seem offended or too discouraged

when Burroughs collected only one glass of whisky from the bar.

"Here y'are, Dilworth," said Burroughs. "Drink that, and then buy yourself three more. I've got to get Stevie back. He's pissed again; it happens quicker and quicker. One of these nights we're not going to make it, and we'll end up in a Scotch jail."

"Say the word," whispered the Scotsman, "and I'll slip oot—never mind the rain—and bring a taxi."

"And the word's a dram, eh? You go and jump over a haggis, wee man. Before I go, Dilworth, let me warn you about this little red-faced pimp. Sure as piss he's going to sell you his respectable woman and her bonny daughter. Take it from a guy that's been, she's sixty and her daughter's damn near forty."

"Civilised hospitality," whispered the Scotsman. "They feed you as well."

"Spam and potatoes," said Burroughs.

"Fish and chips, if you prefer it."

Eager as a neophyte to observe the rituals, Luke had already drunk most of the whisky; but instead of sharing the calmness of the devotees around him, he felt sick and confused. He wanted to rush out into the fresh air, away from the cigarette smoke, the alcoholic smells, the quiet chatter that meant nothing to him, and the even less intelligible laughter.

"They'll dry you," wheedled the Scotsman, "give you supper in front of a good fire, make you comfortable any way you like. Cosy wee hoose in its ain grounds. No interference from neighbours. Cheap too."

"I was forgetting, Dilworth," said Burroughs, gazing into his face. "You prefer them small and old. Met a girl friend of yours once in a taxi. Go ahead then, if that's what you want. Be seeing you."

He went over to the alcove and put his arm round his friend's neck.

"Pair o' pansies, if you ask me," muttered the Scotsman. "Well, what d'you say? Are you on?"

Luke thought he was going to vomit. He made for the door and the gutter outside.

Two women under umbrellas passed, on their way home from a meeting in their church hall.

"Terrible," said one; and the other added, "What would his poor mother think if she could see him now?"

He straightened up, bewildered with shame, and made for home. He did not think about his own mother but, strangely, about young Tommy's who had abandoned him at birth.

Two or three times he stopped, telling himself he must go to Agnes. She would comfort him and he would comfort her. He would tell her Granny was dead. He would tell her that Miss Greenloaning did not want them to get married in the church. He would tell her Tommy had run away. He would tell her he wanted to marry her. He would tell her everything.

But he found himself not at the door of the house where the rabbits lived, but at the door of the house which Ann Plenderleith had said was smelly.

The wind nudged against his legs like an importunate cat. He thought it was Mick and bent down to stroke the poor thing. It was only the wind, and for a few seconds he stooped there, just stroking the wind.

He went into the house. He pressed his brow against Granny's door and murmured, "It's all right, Granny, it's all right," not really knowing what he meant.

In the living-room when he put on the light he was startled to see Granny's chair empty, though he had been expecting to see it empty.

She had not believed in an after-life. She had once pointed to her husband in the photograph. "If he could, Brisbane there would keep a place for me. But he was never able to keep his turn in ony queue. Why should he be different there?"

Mr Brisbane had never looked so woeful.

In his own room as he was putting on dry clothes, including an American cardigan whose poor-quality wool had roused Granny's scorn, he heard noises outside his window. They sounded like footsteps. He heard them again. It could not be Agnes. He had wedged the window tight with specially shaped pieces of wood.

He went to the back door and opened it. Rain beat against his face. Someone was standing there.

"Who is it?" he asked.

He was a man wearing a black hat and holding in front of him a bunch of flowers.

It occurred to Luke it must be Mr Tolmie. These were flowers he had taken to the hospital and sadly had brought back.

Luke felt a great pity for him.

"Is that you, Mr Tolmie?" he said. "Would you like to come in, sir, out of the rain?"

He felt an excitement of joy and hope. The flowers were an offering to him. They were a gesture of kinship.

Agnes and Luke would get married, the baby would be born, and Mr Tolmie, as its grandfather, would be able to feel as he held it in his arms that, whatever disappointments he had suffered, this gift of a child was consolation.

Then the man in the black hat stepped forward. It was Mr Tolmie. Amidst the flowers was a hatchet. He began to strike out **madly**.

PART THREE

LIKE ALL DOUCE well-kirked small Scots towns, what Ardhallow abhorred most was notoriety, and throughout her history she had always managed to avoid it.

In the 1890s a steamer loaded with sacrilegious Glaswegians sailed down the Clyde determined to land on Ardhallow pier though they knew it was closed and padlocked on Sundays by order of the town council. The Ardhallovians who turned out in their hundreds to oppose this desecration did so dressed in Sunday bowlers and bonnets, brandishing nothing more offensive than Bibles and hymn books. The invaders landed, scaled the gates, and took a symbolical stroll along the promenade, assailed with cries of "Shame" and "Gang back to Glesca", but menaced by no fists or stones. The following Sunday, when they came again, this time in pelting rain, they found the gates left open, not in welcome but as a precaution, since they had threatened to bring files. This time their stroll along the front was watched in thoughtful silence.

Before the summer was over regular Sunday sailings had begun to and from the pier, with much added prosperity to the town. A stronghold of the past had been yielded in the Ardhallow way, decently and profitably.

The town's most tremendous test of course had been the coming of the Americans, with their ugly big depôt ship, their submarines armed with nuclear bombs, and their dozens of sailors who, to begin with anyway, fornicated drunkenly with outlandish whores in front gardens among prized roses. Worse than these, though, were the thousands of C.N.D. demonstrators who, from all over the country, had marched with banners to Loch Hallow, where they lay down on the road and had to be dragged by the dozen into Black Marias or vans deputising as such, and taken to the Masonic Hall, where they were fined ten pounds each. Not one Ardhallovian was among them. (Young Ann Plenderlieth, foolish girl, had wanted to be arrested, but her father had nipped in to snatch her away just in time.)

Naturally such commotions could not be kept out of newspapers or off television screens. Ardhallow became for a day or two at a time the most mentioned and photographed town in Scotland; but it quite escaped becoming notorious for the good reason that no one of local importance took part in the unlawful antics.

Ardhallow indeed, modestly but firmly, took the opportunity to make clear to the admiring world that its churches (including St Aidan's, in spite of its minister's reservations), its town council, its Rotary Club, its Masonic Lodge, its British Legion, its Shopkeepers' Association, its taxi-drivers, its publicans, its landladies with houses to rent at American prices—in short, all the community that mattered, were proud their town had been chosen as the base from which Christian civilisation was to be defended. Used contraceptives among the trampled roses, and American women in the main street with plastic curlers in their hair, were a small price to pay for so great and lucrative an honour.

Therefore even at the height of the demonstrations Ardhallow preserved its dignity, thanks to its instinct for what was for its own good, and its aversion to unseemly passion. As one councillor said, no matter what happened, even if an accident did happen on the *Perseus*

—though the President himself had more or less guaranteed that this was impossible—and an H-bomb did go off, blowing the entire town to smithereens, and half of Glasgow, they could still face it with a sense of duty well done.

The bloody murder of the young American sailor by the Ardhallow joiner, followed by the latter's spectacular suicide, on the very night his wife had died of cancer, and the atheistical old landlady of the murdered man had died too, and the orphan Tommy Springburn had decamped from the Home—even all this might not have been too much for the town's canniness to digest if, as Provost McBean himself put it, it hadn't happened all at once, if they hadn't had to gulp it down holus-bolus.

The *Ardhallow Times* did its best to help the town keep its head and reputation by using no bigger headlines than when reporting the town-council debates. Alas, its patriotic self-denial was in vain. Other newspapers, with far wider circulations, used their blackest, thickest, and most sensational headlines.

Through no fault of its own Ardhallow had at last become notorious.

Reporters infested the town, giving good business to those hotels, like the Arms, that kept open during winter. They came convinced that the Scotsman had killed the American because of the Bomb. Conversation with dour natives soon informed them that the truth was simpler and homelier: Tolmie, well-versed in the Old Testament, in a fit of holy madness had killed the man belonging to an outside tribe who had bairned his daughter. This account, however, was considered too parochial, of insufficient world-wide interest, and was played down. Only the *Ardhallow Times*—a sparrow's chirp in that cacophony of macaws—bravely pointed out that Tolmie and his fellow worshippers in the Church of Christ the Master had been the most fervid supporters of the Americans, and

157

more than once had urged them to drop bombs on Russia, without waiting for any other pretext than the abominable atheism of that country.

Three local men were afterwards thought to have let the town down. An opportunity for personal glory, as well as financial gain, was given them, and they seized it too selfishly. In the case of one no one was surprised since he was a chronic disgrace; but the two others, considering their profession, should have shown more restraint and dignity.

These two were Willie Liddlestane, undertaker, and his nineteen-year-old son Jimmy, his apprentice. They had discovered the body of Dilworth when they had gone in the morning to coffin old Nellie Brisbane. The corpse they hadn't bargained for was lying face down outside the back door. "That's to say," Liddlestane was to quaver, to all those reporters in the Arms lounge, "if you could ca' it a face." It seemed there had been a number of seagulls on the drying-green, not far from the body; the Liddlestanes thought they had been feeding on that mutilated face. "Their beaks," said young James, "were all bloody." But many Ardhallovians, who had lived with gulls all their lives, were incredulous. On every gull's beak, they pointed out, was a red spot. This, in the bright sunshine of that shocking morning, could easily have deceived even men with undertakers' nerves. But the bit about the gulls got into newspapers in at least three languages.

The third man was old Donald Tosh. If Ardhallow had ever been asked to choose the citizen it best could do without, he would have received a fair number of votes, including his own perhaps: for he was as daft as he was scandalous.

Yet it was his unwashed runkled hairy face, his junk-carrying barrow, his garden strewn with old car tyres and broken cookers, and his long filthy coat that were portrayed in the newspapers and on television.

Early in the morning, with a barrow-load of junk so useless not even tinkers would have it, old Tosh sneaked to the Sodger's Brig, though dumping there had long been forbidden, with a notice threatening a five-pound fine. While trying to tip out the rubbish he let go one of the handles because of his bad left arm, and in a second junk barrow, and himself went tumbling "erse ower elbow" down the steep bank into the burn where, when he opened his eyes after two or three minutes during which he thought he was dead, he found himself within kissing distance of Will Tolmie's broken face. At first in his bewilderment he imagined Tolmie must have come down with the contents of the barrow. When he had recovered as much of his wits as he could he clambered up the bank in great pain for he had hurt his leg, and hobbled, with snarls at any passer-by showing concern, to the police-station, to report to Sergeant Brownlie, the only policeman in Ardhallow he trusted.

The town council officially discussed the tragedy, and its effect on the town. At first none could see the faintest ray of consolation, not even Bailie Pedderbairn whom a colleague had once accused of being an "optimistic idiot". All agreed it was a very bad thing for the town. For any self-respecting town it would have been bad, but particulary so for Ardhallow which, after all, as a holiday resort, existed to give people pleasure, not to terrify and scunner them.

Councillor Dunmore, owner of a boarding-house, thought that the Americans ought to be made to pay compensation. At first there was the silence of rumination, for the others hadn't forgotten, if he had, that it was an American who'd been murdered. One, to keep the thing going, asked what sort of compensation the councillor had in mind. A swimming pool, he replied at once. Then ex-Provost Balderstone, eighty and irascible, asked sarcastically whether it would be called the Dilworth Pool or the Tolmie Pool. Impervious to sarcasm, especially from a man with less than himself in the bank, Councillor Dunmore remarked that he personally would have no objection if it was called the Johnson Pool, after the President. Wasn't Johnson a Scots enough name?

It was Mrs Hossack, the only woman councillor, who began to cheer them up a little by pointing out that Granny Brisbane's cottage and Sodger's Brig could just as easily attract tourists as repel them. She told them how the folk of Moffat, itself a resort though inland, would say to each other on a fine summer's evening, "Let's go for a walk to Ruxton's Dump," this being a place on the road where a murderer had jettisoned into the bracken a parcel of his victim's chopped-up remains. When she had been there the words "Ruxton's Dump" had been whitewashed on the road; this she thought bad taste, and she hoped that Ardhallow would leave the Brisbane cottage and the brig to speak for themselves.

After another ruminatory silence, they murmured she could be right: human nature was odd. Already dozens of people, including lots of strangers, were flocking to the two places.

It was agreed at the same meeting that Will Tolmie, though a suicide, not to mention a murderer, could be buried in the municipal cemetery, if this was desired by his next of kin. As someone said, the smell of gas there was such that any unnatural resorting to the grave would be discouraged.

The town's kirks were looked to for balm for its wounded soul. What they were not to do was to try and puzzle out, in public, the theological reasons why so hideous a disaster had been heaped on Ardhallow, and not on any one of a hundred towns not a whit more respectable or God-fearing.

From no accepted pulpit therefore, not even from the Free Kirk's, was it as much as hinted that the horrid events might have been a judgement on the town for having given sanctuary, for reasons never honestly examined, to weapons of mass destruction. The Rev. Robert Plenderleith, who did think that, had the sense not to utter it, either to his congregation in public, or to his fiancée in private. The Free Kirk minister, Mr Carradale, however, could not resist saying, to his tiny flock, that a town which allowed putting and golf and similar secularities on the Sabbath ought not to be surprised to find the devil on the rampage in its midst.

On the whole, though, those services at which the horrid events were faced up to were rather wonderful, in that neighbours who on ordinary Sundays merely smiled at one another and noted the newness or otherwise of hats this time looked more closely and saw more deeply. There was an upsurge of loyalty, and indeed affection. They knew, even as it warmed their hearts and wetted their eyes, that it would not last, indeed could not, otherwise the millennium would have arrived before it was due, but they knew also, having lived long enough in the world, that because something was transitory it need not therefore be false.

All those who had come into contact with either the murderer or his victim on the night of the crime had stories to tell, over and over again, to relatives, friends, neighbours, acquaintances, and reporters.

The night sister in the hospital told how embarrassed she had been by Tolmie praying so long at his dead wife's bed. Though there were things to be done, which he was preventing, she had left him alone for quite a while; but she had got nervous after an hour. She had then tried, tactfully, to break into his prayer and persuade him to leave. He had paid no heed. It was only when his daughter Agnes had arrived that he had gone, and very quickly too. He didn't say a single word to the girl, though she'd called to him. Mrs McQuarrie had pictured him going back to his empty house and she had been sorry for him. It had never entered her head he was bent on murder. But then at that time she hadn't known about Agnes being pregnant.

Mrs Dinmont, on duty that night in the reception office, told how the young American had come enquiring for Agnes. He had been soaked and tired. But nobody could have been politer.

Chuck Nelson, after a few whiskies, confided to some of his mates that the poor bastard Dilworth mightn't be the father of the child because of which he'd got hacked to death. "Who is then, Chuck?" they laughed. "You, you horny bugger?" After that he couldn't have convinced them if he'd taken them to the spot and shown them the dogs' shit, so he said nothing and never again alluded to the child.

Most of the men who had been in the pub when Dilworth paid his short visit didn't remember noticing him. But for wee Rab Gilliespie it was a godsend. Men who usually avoided him were willing to pay in drams to listen to his story of how he could have saved Dilworth's life if he had been more successful in his pimping.

Dr Milne, meeting Sergeant Brownlie in the street, said to him, "Tell the truth, Sergeant, were you aware you were in the presence of a doomed man? Did you see a mark on his brow? Did you hear a voice?"

The sergeant gravely answered that he hadn't. Had the doctor?

"No, I did not," he answered, rather crossly, and went off, leaving the sergeant perplexed for the rest of the day.

THE TOWN WAS quickly aware that in the tragedy there was, not a heroine—the word occurred to nobody—but a central character, still alive.

Many previously had heard of Agnes, but very few had known her. Those who had been at school with her were shocked at what had happened, as everyone else was, but some of them added that they weren't really all that surprised: if misfortune was ever to befall Agnes, it was bound to be wholesale and disastrous. She had believed she was the only person in the school, including the teachers, in the Lord's good books, whereas the very opposite had been so obviously the case, *she* was the odd one out as a single glance at her showed. Poor Agnes, nicknamed "Wee Plukey" by Eddie Raitt and his pals, had always been left to herself, in playground and classroom. Most of them remembered having said or thought at the time that one day her peculiar kind of pride would have an appropriately peculiar kind of fall. But, they now admitted, they hadn't quite expected murder and suicide, on top of illegitimacy.

Everybody agreed, with varying degrees of regret, that she was partly to blame. If she hadn't, to use a favourite word of her father's, fornicated with the Yank there would have been no murder and no suicide, not to mention no illegitimacy, and her mother's death might have been put off.

However, most were of the opinion she had been punished enough; indeed, when they came to think seriously about it, in bed trying to go to sleep or feeling a pain that could be wind or heart trouble, they felt that her punishment had been too savage, that this display of the Lord's retributive powers was altogether too tremendous for anybody's peace of mind. Far more fragments of prayer flitted through the minds of Ardhallovians that week than during the previous ten years.

One woman, a member of Tolmie's sect, was heard to say that young Agnes deserved to be stoned to death; but since Mrs Belhaven had previously said that certain shop-keepers should be similarly dealt with for overcharging, no one took her too seriously.

It was hoped that as soon as the mess had been tidied up as much as it ever could be Agnes would find a job somewhere else, preferably in Glasgow where in the blacker shade of turpitude obtaining there her being the daughter of a murderer, and the mother of a bastard whose father had been killed by its grandfather, stood a better chance of not being noticed.

That complexity of evil and misfortune in which she stood involved was often remarked upon, with a reluctant admiration.

To Ardhallow's astonishment and uneasiness a group of people in Glen Canach, led by Miss Breckinridge and Mr McColm the forester, decided, after a meeting in the school there, to let Miss Tolmie know she had their sympathy and support. Miss Breckinridge herself came to Ardhallow with the message. She told Agnes that the children were missing her.

That was true, particularly in the case of Hamish McKendrick. As he chased his classmates round the tree stump in the playground, aiming an imaginary hatchet at their skulls, he assured them that Miss Tolmie would bring back with her the real hatchet and put it in the class museum she had begun, along with the flint arrowheads.

During the days after the discovery of the two bodies Agnes was seldom seen in public. People and reporters waiting outside her uncle's house got only brief glimpses as she hurried into or out of her uncle's taxi. Several times her aunt appeared at the door to order those spec-tators away. Once she carried a bucket of water and yelled that if they were mating dogs she'd throw it over them. They wondered what the hell she meant, and would have been much more offended than they were if they hadn't realised that, as the Tolmie in command, for her man had gone to pieces and wee Agnes was too young and overwhelmed, Sadie had more than enough on her mind to distort it: two corpses to bury, a niece to save from hysteria and miscarriage, a husband to bully into taking control of himself, Sunday newspapers to haggle with over the price of Agnes's story, and the police to satisfy.

It was learned, nobody quite knew how, that old Granny had left Agnes her cottage, worth in those days of inflated prices over three thousand pounds, and its contents, worth no more than fifty pounds, less if dealers were involved, except for one magnificent piece, a sideboard with carvings, made, it transpired, by Will Tolmie himself. Those who saw it in their pilgrimage to see the old woman in her coffin talked more about it afterwards than they did about her. The television set hired by the Yank had been taken away.

Dozens saw Agnes at the old woman's funeral, but only from a distance. Expecting her to weep violently, clutch her hair, shriek, or even fall to the ground in despair, they were all the more moved when instead, dressed neatly in black, she was by far the calmest person there. Her aunt, whom nobody had seen weep ever before, wept. Her uncle kept blowing his nose into a big white hanky: that was his way of weeping. Mr Plenderleith, the minister, was present, but not in that capacity. Granny, it seemed, had stipulated there was to be no religion. So he stood beside fat wee Oliphant, the lawyer—another surprise mourner—and looked oddly huffed, like a football player ready to score half a dozen goals but made to wait in the background.

Luckily it was quite a pleasant day, with no rain and little wind. The smell of gas was bearable.

Those who made the effort to get a closer look at Agnes's

face reported no tears and a weird smile. They were sure she wasn't really aware of what was going on. Her wits had been stunned, like a bird that had flown against a window. God knew if they would ever fly again.

In the male staffroom of the High School, when this apparent stolidity under fearful stress was discussed, it was attributed to lack of imagination. Tales were exchanged of Agnes's incorrigible literalness of mind, and her inabilty ever to see a joke.

A maths master told how when he had once said to a dullard, "Oh, for God's sake, boy, sit down," Agnes, no bright mathematician herself, had waited behind, solemn as Moses, to rebuke him for his blasphemy. "When I told her I truly felt grateful to the Almighty whenever Bonnar, I think his name was, sat down and left me in peace, she stared at me for at least ten seconds and then she said, 'I hope you're telling the truth, sir.' You know, I feel a damn fool even to this day when I remember it. Poor Agnes."

A teacher who had had Agnes in his form class told how, during the twenty minutes set down for religious instruction in the morning, which he spent in checking his work for that day and the class in quietly chatting, an amicable arrangement, he used to be pestered by Agnes wanting to know why he never gave them Bible. One day it occurred to him that since he was shortly to set off to search for the grail of promotion he had better not get the reputation of being anti-religion: nothing in Scotland would more quickly blight his quest.

So, to the disgust and indignation of the rest of the class, he had ordered them to bring Bibles and read them. To give her her due, Agnes had not made too much of her victory.

He told that story against himself to the accompaniment of rueful laughter. It illustrated so well the predicament of the Scottish teacher whose interest in religion was no more or less than that of the Scottish butcher or baker or banker, but who nevertheless was expected to teach it to children to whom, because of the age they lived in, it was utterly meaningless.

They all told, each offering a section of the story, how Agnes had once gone to Mr Falconer, the Rector, and informed him that certain boys, among them Edward Raitt, a pet of his, were calling her "Wee Plukey". Falconer could never take to her because, whenever he caught sight of her in front of him at the school assembly, his religious performance, at best perfunctory, became louder and crosser but no more exalting. So, instead of sympathising with her, he'd been foolish enough to give her a lecture on the meanness of telling tales. She had riposted with one on the folly of not punishing transgressors as they deserved.

Poor Agnes, they agreed shrewdly, was perhaps fortunate in being insulated by that peculiar crassness. After she had recovered from the shock, there was little danger of the horror preying on her mind for months, perhaps for years, as it would with other people. She might even, amongst her dim anachronistic beliefs, make out a divine purpose in what had happened to her, for she had been heard to say, several times, once to the Rector himself, that nothing the Lord did or allowed to happen was purposeless. If that absurd childish conviction remained it might well comfort her, in some incomprehensible way.

3

AMONG THE HANDFUL who got a chance to see Agnes closely was Dora Plenderleith.

She was in her classroom taking a geography lesson when the headmaster knocked at the door and came in. He waited, bald head tilted, for his due, which was the prompt rising to their feet of the thirty-nine eight-year-olds and their hearty chorusing of "Good morning, Mr Spence."

They sat down again, puzzled, looking at one another, and wondering what they had done wrong, for Mr Spence, usually so joky, looked as if he was about to burst out crying. The bit of paper he carried as his excuse for entering a classroom shook like a fan. His voice when he spoke to Miss Plenderleith was hoarse and loud.

To their amusement and her surprise, he took her by the arm and almost dragged her out of the room, closing the door behind them.

One little girl remarked to her neighbour that perhaps the school was on fire.

"Dora," he gasped, "you're a friend of Agnes Tolmie's, aren't you?"

"Well, yes," she said with a smile. "I was at college with her, and at school. Is anything the matter? Don't say her mother's dead?"

"Come to my room, Dora. I must sit down. My legs are shaking."

"But the children—"

"Oh, they'll come to no harm. That's the main thing, Dora, they'll come to no harm."

Usually what worried him was that they would scribble on the desks or make too much noise.

In his room he sat down at his desk and pleaded with her to sit down too.

"I'm not a native of Ardhallow," he said.

He came from Aberdeen; he was an elder of her father's church.

"But I've been here for over twenty years and I'm as fond of the place as if I'd been born here."

"Mr Spence, what's happened?" she asked, now alarmed.

"Dora, five minutes ago I had a phone call from Mrs Spence. She knows I don't like family matters brought up in school time. But this was no family matter; at least, it was a matter that concerns all families in the town, no, in the whole country, for that matter, God help us, in the entire civilised world. She had just had a call herself, from a friend of hers, a lady whose name I must not disclose. Sufficient to say, a most reliable source; the horse's mouth, you might say, in the circumstances. This is no monstrous rumour, Dora, but stark truth."

"What is, Mr Spence?"

"We are among the first to know, outside official circles. Dora, last night—" he paused.

For some reason she remembered Luke's strange visit to the manse.

"Last night Agnes Tolmie's father killed a young American, and then flung himself from Sodger's Brig; he's dead too."

She felt as if icy water was being poured inside her dress.

"To make matters more dreadful still, Mrs Tolmie died last night, in the hospital. Do you see now why I had to speak to someone?"

She too wanted to speak to someone. Not to Edward, who would try to make a joke even of this. Not to Elizabeth, who would be too ready to throw common sense over it, like a blanket over a fire. Not to any of her colleagues who would be struck dumb. To her father. She wanted then so much to speak to him that tears of relief came into her eyes.

"You're her friend, Dora. It's hit you even harder than it's done me."

Only then did Dora consider Agnes's plight. With a whimper she remembered Agnes on the ferry that day of blue skies and sunshine crying how lucky she was, and believing it. She remembered too that Agnes was pregnant. Only then did it occur to her that the man Mr Tolmie had killed must be Luke.

"Who was he?" she whispered. "The American? Do they know?"

"I believe he was courting Agnes. Mr Tolmie, a very strict man I understand, did not approve. But he must have gone mad."

"Luke?" she whispered.

Mr Spence gazed about.

"His name's Luke Dilworth."

"Do you know him, Dora?"

"He was at the manse last night. About eight. Elizabeth took him home."

"Forgive me, Dora. If I'd known you were personally involved I would never have told you. But of course it will all come out. Would you like to go and see Agnes, now? I thought myself I would, every decent person would want to, but we don't know her, we wouldn't know what to say. You'll have to be brave, Dora. But you are."

She didn't want to go. She had never really understood or liked Agnes. It wasn't likely she would understand her any better now when she was deranged by grief.

"What about my class?" she asked.

"I'll see it's looked after. In any case, it's only twenty minutes till the lunch break."

She went, in her red Mini, by the sea front. It was twice as far that way, but she wanted a sight of the sea, wide and shining, to save her mind from becoming narrow and dark. Gulls stood on the iron rail along the promenade. They rose as she passed, with urgent squawking, as if they were trying to tell her something and were contemptuous because she didn't know it already. They were so simple in their lives.

She tried to concentrate on familiar simple things: the key ring her father had given her, an old man exercising his dog. But her mind kept skidding into horror. Desperately she thought of Edward, Ann, and her father. How close madness really was. If the gulls' simplicity was sanity everybody was mad.

The road and house were as quiet and ordinary as on any other day. The blinds weren't even drawn. There was no cross marked in blood on the door; only the bronze knocker shaped like a rabbit's head.

As she waited on the doorstep she wondered if Agnes's aunt would open the door and, wearing the apron of blessed every-day normality, ask her calmly what she wanted.

She had never taken to Mrs Tolmie, whom she thought too hard in her views of people and too proud of that hardness. Therefore when the door opened and she saw those eyes red with weeping but still hard and proud she knew for certain that Mr Spence hadn't been having a demented dream.

"I'm Dora Plenderleith," she said. "Is Agnes here?"

"I ken who you are. Aye, she's here."

"So it's true?"

"Is it oot then?"

The hall was much too narrow, the ceiling too low. This was not the kind of house in which to have to endure such terrible knowledge in one's head. But would inside St Aidan's itself, so spacious and high, be any better? Or on top of Ben More, the highest hill in the district?

"What *did* happen, Mrs Tolmie? I'm not sure. I just heard about ten minutes ago."

"You came quick. Tolmie killed him with a hatchet, and then threw himself from Sodger's Brig. Pity he didn't do that first. He had flowers with him."

Dora didn't understand that last remark. But who in these circumstances could talk sense?

"Was it Luke Dilworth?"

"It was."

"I was told Agnes's mother—"

"She's dead too. The three of them are lying side by

side in the hospital mortuary. Archie's with the police. They're still putting things together."

"How is Agnes?"

"Feeding the rabbits. She said she'd do it and she's doing it."

"Feeding the rabbits?" But then what could be done that would make less incredible and more bearable this knowledge in the head? "How is she?"

"Just step in here, will you, Miss Plenderleith?"

She opened the door of what Dora took to be the best room, kept for show. It had black-and-orange furniture. On the sideboard were silver cups, and a big white rabbit under a glass cover.

"I'll tell her you're here," said Mrs Tolmie.

"But what am I to say to her?"

Mrs Tolmie waited at the door; she wasn't keen to go and bring Agnes.

"Shouldn't you be at school?" she asked. "It's not dinner-time yet."

"I got away."

They knew the subject was absurd but they wanted to go on with it.

"Here she is." Mrs Tolmie stepped quickly back into the room, behind the orange-and-black settee. She seemed almost afraid; so much so that when Agnes came in she muttered something and rushed out.

Yet Agnes was calm. In contrast to Dora's, plucking at a handkerchief, her hands were at peace; it was easy to imagine them patiently feeding the rabbits. She was wearing a dark green dress and looked prettier than Dora had ever seen her before, and somehow cleaner. Her weeks in Glen Canach had done her good. Her skin was clear, her hair had a lustre, and her eyes, which had often struck Dora as sly, were childlike in their frankness.

If she had been weeping sorely and had begged Dora to help her, Dora would not have been more moved, and more disturbed. Agnes, she thought, had simply rejected what had happened. Brought up to regard as wickedness the playing of football on Sundays, she had been utterly unable to apprehend this gigantic evil of murder and suicide. She had convinced herself it hadn't happened.

Dora jumped up, and, weeping, embraced Agnes. She thought of Edward whom she loved, whom she would marry, but whom she would never quite trust.

"I'm sorry, Agnes. I'm terribly sorry."

Agnes ended the embrace, gently but firmly. She was still dry-eyed. She sat down on the settee.

"I loved my father," she said, slowly and carefully, like someone saying something in a foreign language.

Dora remembered Elizabeth saying that one of the disadvantages of an upbringing like Agnes's was that it had kept her at a distance from ordinary human affection. Dora had thought it a callous thing to say, but true.

"When somebody you love does something bad, what do you do?"

Dora shook her head, unable to answer.

"When your Ann was taking part in all those demonstrations you didn't stop loving her, did you?"

Dora felt too confused and full of pity to be angry.

"And there's Edward. Look at his faults, and yet you still love him. He failed in his exam, didn't he?"

Was this equating of marching in demonstrations and failing in exams with murder and suicide deliberate, a kind of defensive cunning? Or were Agnes's moral standards really so weird?

Dora could not resist murmuring: "He passed his re-sit."

"That's what I've got to do, Dora: remember my love for my father."

Dora wondered if it was the grim-faced aunt who had given that sane but difficult advice.

"And for Luke too," added Agnes. "If I keep remem-

173

bering I loved them it will be all right. It's not for me to judge."

Dora saw then what Agnes's game was, if it was fair to call it that. She was acting the part of the perfect Christian: forgive for the sake of love; let God judge. If she could keep it up she would be invulnerable.

"I'm going to ask your father to conduct the service at the funeral," said Agnes.

Elizabeth won't let him, thought Dora.

"I trust him," said Agnes, smiling.

Then to Dora's relief the outside door opened and people came in. Men's voices were heard.

Mrs Tolmie looked in. "The police are back," she said.

Dora got to her feet. "I'll have to be going."

"Thanks for coming," said Agnes. "Mention it to your father, will you? I'll get in touch with him."

Dora involuntarily shook her head. "It's Ann, you see," she explained. "She's not to be excited. We haven't told her about Tommy yet."

"Why, what's happened to him?"

"Didn't you know? He's run away. He's been away all night."

Uncle Archie appeared; he looked as if he had been weeping.

"Superintendent Mitchell wants to ask you a few questions, Agnes," he said. "I've told them everything, but they still want to know."

"Shouldn't we have a lawyer?" asked his wife. "Ring for Oliphant, Archie. He's not much use but he's better than nothing."

"I don't need a lawyer," said Agnes. "I'm not afraid to answer their questions."

Mrs Tolmie saw Dora out, past the two solemn detectives, hats in hands.

"Well, what d'you think of her?" she muttered, at the door. "Can she keep it up?"

Dora wasn't sure whether she meant the genuine Christian attitude or the brave but dangerous sham.

4

When he heard the news Mr Plenderleith's instant reaction was to blame himself: if he had shown a little Christian charity he could have prevented poor Luke's death.

"He was soaked to the skin, Dora. We did not make him as welcome as we should. He sat uneasily among us, in that very chair. I let him leave. I sent him away, on a night of pitiless rain, to a house in which an old woman lay dead."

"But, Dad, you didn't know Granny was dead."

His conscience refused to accept so easy a let-out.

"If I had known would I have asked him to stay? I do not think I would."

"You would if Elizabeth hadn't been here."

That was the bitterest thing he had ever heard Dora say. Wincing, he pretended not to notice the insinuation. She saw the wince and the pretence. Their faces were too easy to read. They knew the truth about each other and were not comfortable.

"We are all involved, Dora," he murmured. "If we are not resolute in loving one another this dreadful crime could diminish us all."

"It hasn't diminished Agnes."

"You speak as if you wished her to be."

"She's to blame, isn't she, partly anyway? She knew better than anybody the kind of man her father was."

"Do you wish the poor girl to be punished?"

"No, I don't. I want her to show some feeling."

"Shock often makes people appear abnormally calm."

"That's not it. Well, I don't think it is."

"Surely you're not accusing her of monstrous callousness?"

"I don't know."

"If ever a human being deserved our compassion, surely poor Agnes does?"

All the same, as he walked among the pines in the manse garden, the minister could not deny himself the atavistic satisfaction of considering whether Tolmie might have been, not mad, as everyone would think, but rather sane in a way too strong and absolute for today's effete humanity.

From childhood Tolmie had feared God and honoured His laws. He had brought up his only daughter in that same inexorable faith. She had sinned, become with child illicitly. He believed—the Bible in a dozen places was his authority—that her debaucher must be punished, not for personal vengeance, but to preserve the purity of his relationship with God.

As he listened to Elizabeth talking about "a sordid spasm of insanity that, thank God, would soon be forgotten", he was tempted to startle her with his own sterner and nobler conception. But he refrained.

She advised him not to take the service at the graveside. She thought too much of him, she said, to give her reasons.

He rang up Edgar Oliphant in his office in the main street, above the stationer's.

"As a man who knows the mind of the world, Edgar, what would you advise?"

"As an elder of your kirk, Robert, I agree with Elizabeth. Best keep clear. None of the Tolmies was ever connected with St Aidan's. You can honourably refuse. If you don't you could find yourself in a trap. How does a Christian minister forgive a murder in public? And you couldn't very well bury him without forgiving him. Remember, there'll be hundreds there, including reporters. To be frank, Robert, I doubt very much if you're the man for a job like this. You've got a reckless streak in you. You might come out with something you'd regret for the rest of your ministerial life."

Thrilled by the unintentional compliment, Robert thanked him and immediately rang up another elder, less worldly than Edgar in spite of his occupation. This was Provost McBean. He did not know it but all through the conversation the Provost was holding a lettuce in his other hand.

The greengrocer always spoke as if his mouth was full of peach juice.

"Sure, Robert, take it on. For the sake of the town. Here's a God-sent opportunity for damping down the sensationalism. Nothing out of the ordinary, just let those outsiders know we're a decent law-abiding God-fearing community. Is it our fault there are bombs in Loch Hallow that could wipe out half the world? They'll make out, you wait and see, that our streets are littered with corpses. Whereas the truth is we've got streets as clean as any in Scotland. Speak up for the town, Robert. You've got it in you. If your sermons are usually on the tame side we know the reasons for that. You've got fire bottled up in you. Use it to cauterise this wound on our body politic. They're telling me, as provost, I should do it. But what's a letter in the *Glasgow Herald* or the *Scotsman* compared with a few right words at the graveside, in the heart of the town?"

It was the reckless streak in him, a flame from the bottled-up fire, that made him, when Agnes telephoned, suggest St Aidan's as the trysting-place.

She agreed without fuss; indeed, she was enthusiastic.

Dora, though, was scandalised. "In the church?" she cried.

It saddened him that his own daughter, now twenty-one, did not understand why, when faced with the greatest challenge of his pastoral life, he should have chosen to meet it in his church.

"For me there is no holier place," he murmured.

Never had she felt so strongly that a thing was utterly wrong, and yet she did not know how to condemn it. She could hardly call her father a dupe and Agnes a dangerous temptress.

"Just the two of you?" she asked.

"Well, this is Wednesday, John Langmuir's evening for practising. I thought the music might help."

"To do what?"

Again he felt disappointed in her. "Need you ask that, Dora? To comfort the poor girl."

She almost said Agnes didn't need comforting; but it would have been ridiculous.

"I'll go with you," she said.

"What about Ann?"

"She'll be all right for half an hour. She plays her piano for hours without noticing whether we're there or not."

"Won't she ask where we're going?"

"We've lied to her before. We'd just have to lie again."

He sighed. How much he had disliked those therapeutic lies, to use Elizabeth's kind word.

"Ring up Elizabeth," said Dora. "After all, she knows Agnes better than you do."

He felt subtly reluctant. "She may be busy."

"Ask her anyway. I think she'd want you to."

"Very well, Dora. I shall ask her."

He asked, and for a quarter of a minute there was no answer. Elizabeth was thinking.

"In the church?" she said, quietly.

"Yes, Elizabeth. It seems to me as good a place as any."

"I don't wish to interfere, Robert, but couldn't she go to the manse?"

"There's Ann."

"I'm afraid Ann must know some time. But the manse is a big house."

"I'd rather not."

"Well, couldn't you go to her uncle's?"

He began to feel slightly indignant. "There was a time, my dear, when there would have been no question as to a church being the best of places in which to pray for strength to overcome dreadful misfortune."

There was a pause.

"I see. All right, I'll meet you there."

She was there before him. Her car was parked outside. She was talking to John Langmuir, the organist. The latter, when he saw the minister, said that he'd be leaving early: he'd promised his wife.

Robert suspected Elizabeth had hinted. She was, however, at her most charming and efficient. She had never before kissed him in public, but she did it then, with Langmuir watching. She was wearing her mink coat which had cost nine hundred pounds. It was no doubt far from her intention to neutralise, as it were, the spirituality of the atmosphere in the dimly lit church. But that was what she was doing.

"Don't let us interfere with your playing, John," she said.

She took Robert's arm and slowly walked with him up the aisle to the back of the church.

"Have you seen the evening paper?" she asked.

"No."

"Horrible headlines, I'm afraid. And pictures. But at least the police seem satisfied that Tolmie did it."

"Was there ever any doubt?"

"It was on television of course. Do you know who represented Ardhallow? That old rascal Tosh, and his rubbish."

They listened to the solemn music.

Elizabeth spoke urgently.

"Robert, darling. This, as you've said, is as good a place as any. I would like us to fix a definite date for our wedding."

"I thought we'd agreed on the spring," he said, taken aback.

"I'd prefer earlier. Before Christmas. I lose confidence, Robert. It may not seem so, but I do. I wonder sometimes if you really want to marry me."

"Elizabeth, my dear, how can you say so?" He tried to speak with the same urgency. "I want it very much."

"Early December then. There's nothing stopping us, is there?"

"Of course not."

"It means a great deal to me, Robert. I love you. I want to have the right to be with you always."

To keep me, he thought far away in his mind, from meeting girls you don't like in my church.

She liked expensive scents. It was pervading the whole church.

In that same remote part of his mind he saw in her what Ann disliked and Dora distrusted, but much closer he saw that with her supporting and pushing him he could quickly ascend a pulpit in a fashionable quarter of Edinburgh or Glasgow and become, what he had always wanted to be and what he was confident he could be, an influence in the spiritual life, not merely of a small seaside town, but of the whole country.

From the front of the church near the north door they heard a voice: "Mr Plenderleith?"

It was Agnes's.

"Let me," murmured Elizabeth, and she set off, taking her scent with her.

Her footsteps could be heard punctuating the music.

Robert shivered. The church was chilly. He prayed that Elizabeth would be tactful at least.

Elizabeth was happy; her pity therefore was more tender than it would have been. She put her gloved hands on Agnes's shoulder and looked into her face.

"Oh Agnes, my dear," she whispered, and embraced the girl as well as she could considering the bulkiness of the fur coat.

Suddenly the organ was silent. Langmuir was heard moving his stool.

"I can't tell you how terribly sorry I am," murmured Elizabeth, "how sorry we all are."

After about half a minute she was pushed back, not so gently.

"It was Mr Plenderleith I came to see," said Agnes.

The minister heard. So did the organist now descended, putting on his coat.

Elizabeth had compassion. She was not offended. Her voice was still rich and strange with pity.

"He's here," she said. "I came too. I hope you don't mind, Agnes. I wanted to tell you how sorry I am."

Agnes did not reply. She made for the minister at the back of the church.

Elizabeth would not allow herself to feel snubbed. She remembered the ordeal the unfortunate girl must be going through. She thought Agnes's calm ominous.

John Langmuir passed her on his way out. "Good night, Elizabeth," he said. Then he called, "Good night, Robert."

"Good night, John. I'll lock up."

"Good night, Miss Tolmie. May I add my sincere sympathy?"

"Thank you, Mr Langmuir," answered Agnes, in a voice so humble and sweet that Elizabeth with a pang could not help contrasting it with the cold and rather harsh voice Agnes had used to her.

She sat down in the nearest pew. Agnes, she felt sure, had not been deliberately unfriendly. In her state of mind she would hardly know what tone of voice she was using.

Robert was glad Elizabeth had decided to stay at a distance. He intended to offer up a prayer on Agnes's behalf. What he wanted to say Elizabeth would have regarded as too fundamental. She said it was a tendency he had.

"Hello, Agnes," he said.

He took her hand and pressed it. Had he known how more than once he had been included in her masturbatory fantasies, he might not have pressed quite so warmly. After his hand let go her hand still clung; but he thought nothing of it.

"This must have been a dreadful day for you, poor Agnes," he murmured.

Elizabeth frowned, smiled, then frowned again as she realised they were going to speak so quietly that she would not be able to hear without great straining. She did not want to hear but she ought not to be excluded. So she kept frowning. At the same time, she was pleased it was Robert and not her who was to do the comforting. She knew too quickly when she had stumbled into artificiality: it dried her up. Robert, bless him, was never aware of it, though he did it oftener.

He felt as if a great and holy opportunity had been given to him.

"Shall we sit down?" he whispered. "You must be tired."

They sat down. Agnes kept very close. He understood. The very vastness and emptiness of the kirk would in itself have caused her to seek closeness, but there was in addition the terror of loneliness that the deaths in the one day of her father, mother, neighbour and lover must have left her in.

"Will you pray for me, Mr Plenderleith?" she whispered.

"With all my soul, Agnes."

But he could not, as he was accustomed, clasp his hands

in front of him, the better to concentrate. Very shyly Agnes took his right hand and held it tightly, like a child. He felt her tremble with the fear that must be in her, and indeed might remain in her for the rest of her life. His prayer could scarcely exorcise it, however inspired.

Elizabeth did not move or speak or even sigh, but he was aware of her all the time. Therefore his prayer to some extent was inhibited after all; certainly it was curtailed.

Little Agnes, though, pressing his hand and sighing her approbation, gave him as much encouragement as she could.

"Lord, we sit here in Thy house, conscious as we have never been before that Thy will must be done; and when done borne by us Thy children with humility, without bitterness, and above all with hope. A terrible thing has befallen us in our little town. Its burden lies most heavy on Thy servant Agnes, who prays beside me. Thou knowest how all her young life she has devotedly followed Thy ways, often in the face of much discouragement."

Elizabeth coughed. Yet surely she was too far to hear.

He continued: "Upheld by her faith, let her be an example to us all, of courage in the face of greatest adversity. In the old days when men were blinded as to Thy compassionate purpose girls as young and tender in years as Agnes were put to death in Thy service. In the midst of the flames they astonished and inspired the beholders by the sweetness of their acceptance. In the midst of her travail let Agnes too astonish and inspire us."

Again Elizabeth coughed. Something seemed to be tickling her throat. Or perhaps she was taking a cold.

"Amen," he said.

"Amen," said Agnes; she sounded a little disappointed. He tried to take his hand back, but did not succeed.

"Thank you, Mr Plenderleith," she murmured. "I feel stronger now."

183

"Hold on to faith, Agnes, and you will never feel weak."

Another cough from Elizabeth.

"Will you take the service?" asked Agnes.

"Yes, Agnes, I will."

"They are to be buried together."

"Of course."

"Only my uncle, my aunt and myself will be at the graveside."

He felt a little uneasy at her business-like tone.

"Won't your father's friends in his own church wish to attend?"

"No. They say he's a murderer."

"I see." So he was of course. Must so brutal a fact be kept in mind always, by the dead man's daughter, and by the minister speaking at the graveside? Robert was quite unable to say.

"So they don't want to come," said Agnes.

"I see. But your mother must have had many friends."

"Some of them think she shouldn't be buried with my father."

"I see." So he did, and yet he felt more mystified than ever in his life before. He had expected Agnes to be strange, after such blows; but not so strange as this. She seemed to have more authority than Elizabeth.

"I hope," she said, in her briskest voice yet, "you won't think me impertinent if I ask that Miss Greenloaning shouldn't come."

"I don't think it arises," he said, startled.

"That's all right then. I wouldn't want to hurt her feelings."

He remembered Dora saying she wished Agnes had shown more feeling. His uneasiness grew. He could not truthfully say he thought her in a state of shock; and though she still clung to his hand he wasn't so sure now that she was tormented by fears. She seemed to know too well what she wanted.

He had a sinking feeling that this remarkable girl must have found his prayer inadequate.

Elizabeth suddenly stood up.

"Well," she called, in a voice carefully cleared of the slightest trace of irritation, "can we go now? It's icy in here, Robert. Agnes isn't very warmly clad."

"I'm not a bit cold," said Agnes.

They rose. Slipping out of the pew he tried, tactfully, to shake off her hand; again without success. He hesitated therefore, but she with the greatest confidence took him with her towards Elizabeth. At the very last second she let go his hand. He wasn't sure whether Elizabeth had seen.

"Did you walk, Agnes," asked Elizabeth, "or did your uncle bring you?"

"I walked."

"Then either Mr Plenderleith or I will run you back."

"No, thank you. I'll walk. It isn't far."

They went out together into the street. As Robert locked the door Elizabeth examined Agnes's face in the lamp-light. The smile on it baffled her. It wasn't a happy smile —how could it be?—but it wasn't a miserable one either. She had never seen a smile like it.

"Are you sure you wouldn't like a run home, Agnes?" she asked.

"Yes, I'm sure. Well, thank you, Mr Plenderleith. My uncle will be in touch with you. By the way, how is Ann? Does she know about Tommy yet?"

"No, not yet."

"Ann is fine," said Elizabeth, briskly. "She's going to be able to go to Edinburgh after all."

"I'm glad. She'll be able to see Edward there. They get on well, don't they? Pity he believes in nothing. Good night."

They watched her walk lightly away.

"Is her head turned, do you think?" asked Elizabeth. "It would be no wonder."

He said nothing.

"I'm not going to ask what you and she said to each other in there, I suppose it was private, but I must say she doesn't look like a girl whose father has just killed her lover."

He loved and respected her, he was going to marry her, they would grow old and honoured together, but at that moment he hated her, for representing, as he had done himself for too long, conventional Christianity that took no risks and therefore wrought no miracles.

"How can we tell how such a girl should look?" he said. "It seems to me she is bearing up as if sustained by faith. Why should we be surprised when we find a life-long faith does sustain?"

She thought he was talking nonsense, but pardonable nonsense, so she said, fondly, "Why indeed, my dear?"

Then with affectionate good-nights they went to their respective cars.

5

THERE WAS ONE extra at the graveside. This was Miss Breckinridge who invited herself. She simply picked up the telephone and told Agnes's uncle, as far as he could be told, he havered so much, that she intended to be present. She did not wait for him to consent or to consult anyone.

Nor did she seek permission from the Director of Education to shut her school for the afternoon. Most teachers, she had long ago decided, were sheep, too easily bullied and driven by the dogs of authority; so she had always used her own initiative whenever she saw a need. The barkings from head office had, as the years passed, changed to resigned growls and finally to peevish whimpers. If she had asked for permission it would have been refused, with much palaver; so she didn't ask.

She told the children where she was going. They approved, particularly as they were getting an unexpected half-holiday out of it. They wanted to know if she would be bringing Miss Tolmie back with her. Not yet, she replied; but she was sure Miss Tolmie would return soon.

She was sure of it in spite of a telephone call from Elizabeth Greenloaning. There was going to be a vacancy shortly in Ardhallow Primary, and it might be a good thing for Agnes to be given it, so that she could live with her relatives. Elizabeth had implied that she could arrange for Agnes to be offered the post. Doubtless she could, having the ear of influential men, such as that fat local potentate, Edgar Oliphant.

Miss Breckinridge did not want to attend the funeral. She disliked cemeteries, and was determined to be cremated herself. But she felt she ought to support her young colleague whom she had come, not exactly to like, but to feel fascinated by. As she drove to Ardhallow in her fifteen-year-old Morris Minor, in a deluge of rain, she had to admit to herself that part of the reason for the journey was a desire to find out what effect the ghastly deaths had had upon Agnes's blitheness of spirit, or rather, for that bright word hardly suited so insignificant looking a girl, her unaccountable self-confidence. Miss Breckinridge had not been able to make up her mind if it was the Lord at work, or if it was merely an exceptional example of that evasion of reality which many Christians confused with religion.

She recalled the conversation she had overheard yesterday. It had taken place round the tree stump in the playground.

Hamish McKendrick had wanted to talk about the hatchet; it would be kept, he cried, in a box lined with cotton wool.

Mary McBride, at eleven and a half the oldest in the school, shut him up. "That's not what we're talking about," she said. "We're talking about whether we want Miss Tolmie to come back. Well, do we?"

"Aye, we do," the others cried.

"She'll not be shy," said Mary.

"Oh no." They laughed, as if shy was the last thing they expected Miss Tolmie to be.

"But she could be a bit nervous," said Mary. "Remember, it was a real murder."

They remembered that all right. They had read the papers and watched the television.

"And she's going to have a baby," said Jenny McTurk, whose mother was pregnant.

"I've never seen her nervous," said Fiona McTaggart.

"Nobody has," said Mary. "But that was before her father killed the American."

"With a hatchet," yelped Hamish.

"What I'm trying to say," said Mary, "is that we'll maybe have to help her."

"How can you help a teacher?" asked Duncan Lamont, a dunce, but respected as an excellent swimmer.

"Well, to begin with, Duncan," said Mary, "you can stop laughing when she's singing hymns."

"But it's the way she looks up at the ceiling, where Hamish stuck the gum."

"She's looking at the Lord," said Hamish, with another yelp.

"She's funny," maintained Duncan.

"We know that," said Mary. "But you're the only one that laughs out loud. You'll have to stop it. And when she's taking P.E. nobody's to giggle. I mean you especially, Angus."

Angus McFarlane, dour collector of comics—he had over a hundred—was indignant.

"I'm not the only one," he said.

"It's her shorts," said Duncan. "They're so wide a hedge-hog could run up them."

They laughed.

"She doesn't know she's funny," said Fiona. "That's what I like."

The rest admitted they liked it too.

"Anyway," said Jenny, "if she's going to have a baby she'll not be able to do P.E."

"Her belly will be too big to bend," said Hamish.

Miss Breckinridge thought it time then to rush out and ring the bell. She was three minutes early and they noticed it, with some indignation.

Spray flying from her wheels as she drove through many puddles, she went straight to the cemetery. The rain was of true Ardhallovian relentlessness. Gutters raced, cataracts poured down from faulty pipes, pavements were burns, street corners were desolations, and houses looked as if they were under the sea.

It should have been a satisfactory day for such a funeral; nobody should have been about. But to her great annoyance at the gates of the cemetery and inside it were many people, under umbrellas. She was sure she saw a ghoulish look on all their faces, including those of the two police-men. It did occur to her for an instant that they might be braving the downpour in order to show respect for the dead woman and pity for the dead man, but she dismissed it as sentimental nonsense.

Ardhallow folk had learned to enjoy themselves though very wet. Almost every August their Highland Games, at which world championships were decided, in piping and dancing, were conducted in storms of rain. Nevertheless people turned out in their thousands to applaud with morose loyalty.

She noticed men with cameras. Perhaps the funeral would be shown that night on millions of screens, if the editors concerned thought it newsworthy enough. She felt angry but knew that if she protested she would be in a very small minority. Ardhallow people, like people everywhere nowadays, would think it an honour for their town to be shown on television, even if the occasion was the burial of a local murderer. By passionately preferring privacy and anonymity she proved herself a freak. She was the only one in Glen Canach without a television set. Even the children pitied her.

In her car parked near the gate she put on her goloshes. Then she waited for the hearse and mourners. They arrived on time to the minute. Liddlestane in his weekly advertisements in the local *Times* stressed his punctuality. Miss Breckinridge was surprised to see two coffins, though she had known there would be two. There were only three mourners, if Mr Plenderleith was not counted.

Miss Breckinridge emerged, put up her umbrella, and strode through the gate, not minding how much she jostled those hurrying through with her. Most of these halted at what they considered a decent distance from the grave. She walked on, among the rudest, and reached the grave minutes before the coffins and the Tolmies.

The gravediggers, capes over their heads, paid her no heed. She might have been one of the many stones with which the place was so symmetrically dotted. It was no graveyard to bury a poet in, she thought. It was a school-mistress's idea of a graveyard, very tidy, regular, with nowhere a trace of individuality.

You could have floated a toy yacht in the bottom of the grave. The earth had been neatly heaped ready to be flung back in; the rain had turned it to glaur. She noticed a very healthy-looking worm. Despite the rain there was still a faint smell of gas; it could have been the stink of all the bones under the earth. She felt depressed, and was angry with herself for giving in so quickly. She had come to defy this muck of death and here she was, in less than ten minutes, grueing.

The first coffin arrived—it was the woman's—and was carefully set down on a tarpaulin placed in readiness. Then the four undertaker's men went back for the other at the proper pace, wasting no time but showing no disrespectful haste.

Miss Breckinridge did not know Agnes's aunt, but she had heard of her, and at once recognised the bitter mouth and eyes resentful of their own weeping.

The taxi-driver, at whose letters in the paper Miss Breckridge had often snorted, was that saddest of sights, a braggart reformed; he just couldn't look humble enough.

She nodded curtly to them both.

Robert Plenderleith she liked as a man but did not admire as a minister: his ambitions were too worldly. Otherwise why should he want to marry Miss Greenloaning, that eminent châtelaine. Now in the cemetery he was trying hard to look brave and Christian, and hoping everybody noticed. She let him know with a quick nod that she had noticed. He smiled gratefully.

She went close to Agnes.

"How are you?" she asked, grimly.

It was a foolish question, but in that place, at that time, anyone who tried to say anything at all was bound to be a fool.

In black, with a black veil, Agnes looked pale but not heart-broken. She had not been weeping, like her aunt, and was not weeping now, like her uncle. Though she was so small, and though Miss Breckinridge at that moment vividly remembered her leaping absurdly in those shorts so wide a hedgehog could run up them, she had an undoubted dignity. Her eyes, by no means frantic, took in the headmistress, her uncle and aunt, the minister, the coffin arrived and the coffin arriving, the water in the grave, the glaur, the sky thick with cloud, the rain, and the spectators under their umbrellas; but they seemed to see something else, in compensation, though what it could be Miss Breckinridge didn't dare even to guess.

As she listened to the minister's humdrum prayer, almost drowned by the drumming of rain on umbrellas, and punctuated by the squawkings of gulls, the headmistress wondered. Was she confronted, in the person of Agnes, with the solution to the whole human predicament, if only she could interpret it? Was this calmness in the face of extreme tribulation the consequence of faith, of ineradicable belief that Christ was with her, and with all people, so that life had a purpose and that purpose was good? Or was it a consummate exhibition of that human failing which would destroy the race, refusal to face up to the dirty truth, and eagerness to be deceived by hope however specious?

Miss Breckinridge could not tell. She hoped for all their sakes Christ was at work, but feared it was deception. The minister's words were absolutely no help.

She did not, like the others, throw a little earth on top of the coffins: not because she'd have dirtied her gloves, but because, with her mind so undecided, she distrusted the symbolism of the act.

"Come up to the house, Miss Breckinridge," muttered the aunt. She was weeping. "For something to eat."

"Thank you, no. I want to get home before the road's flooded."

"Isn't this rain terrible? Is it a judgement, d'you think?"

"I do not."

"Yesterday, when auld Granny was buried, it was dry."

The uncle approached. He looked desperate. Miss Breckinridge thought he was going to pour out all his grief and horror and disappointment. Perhaps he did.

"D'you ken, you wouldn't believe it, somebody's painted on my taxi, in yellow letters, this size, 'Tolmie's Hearse'? Is that funny?"

She didn't know what he was talking about.

"Tell you this, laugh if you like, I've got mair pleasure out of my rabbits than ever I did out of people."

Agnes took Miss Breckinridge's arm. "Thanks for coming," she said.

Tell me, Agnes, the headmistress wanted to ask, beside that grave now being discreetly filled in, tell me, if you can, is it really the Lord Himself that's giving you this sweetness? Or have you just been blessed with the right kind of stupidity?

The minister approached. "It was very good of you to come, Miss Breckinridge. I'm sure Agnes appreciated it."

They watched Agnes walk with a strange lightness of foot towards the car. Beside her her aunt trudged as if with a great invisible burden on her back. Perhaps, though, it wasn't so invisible. Agnes's lack of burden was much harder to see.

"Is it shock, d'you think?" asked Miss Breckinridge.

"Partly, of course. But hasn't she been brought up from infancy to believe utterly and without question in Christ?"

"In Jehovah more likely," thought Miss Breckinridge, but did not say it.

"She has had a lifetime of training in faith," said the minister. "Why should we be surprised to find that it had prepared her to face blows that would have shattered others not so strongly propped?"

"Are you surprised then?"

He sighed. "This is not a religious age, Miss Breckinridge. Faith is considered too simple an explanation. Doubt infects us all."

"I think they're waiting for you."

The big black car, a Rolls-Royce, was making no rude impatient noise, but the driver was in his seat, Liddlestane was beside him, and the three Tolmies sat in the back. The hearse had already gone.

"Good afternoon," said Mr Plenderleith, and sadly walked away.

She thought one of the spectators yelled derision, but it was only a gull.

As she walked past those spectators she felt an arrogant superiority over them. It was her kind of stupidity, but she did not rebuke it.

She was in her car taking off her goloshes when she noticed a policeman looking in.

She opened the window about three inches.

"Shouldn't I be parked here?" she asked, impudently.

"That's all right, Miss Breckinridge," he said.

"So I'm known to the law?"

He smiled. "I'm Sergeant Brownlie."

"Well, if I'm not parked in an illegal place, what is it I've done?"

"I'd like your help."

She waited.

"Maybe you've heard a boy's missing from the Home?"

"I have. One of your policemen came to the glen two days ago. We thought he was daft. It's a good twenty miles from Ardhallow, with mountains all the way."

"We thought there was an outside chance he might have been on his way to visit Miss Tolmie."

"Did Agnes know him?"

"It seems so. But of course she wasn't there that night."

"No. Well, sergeant, we'll keep a look-out. My children will look in every hollow tree. Why did he run away in any case? In this day and age cruelty's not allowed in such places. We who are asked to look after other people's children are required to be a lot more tolerant and reasonable than parents."

"He's got no parents. He's a foundling."

"Well, isn't there a school of thought that says the family's a bad institution for the rearing of children: either it spoils them with too much indulgence, or neglects them shamefully? Those that think that would say he's lucky."

He looked puzzled and a bit displeased. He was a good enough man but stupid. There were all kinds of stupidity.

"Let's hope he turns up soon," she said.

As she drove away she felt meaner in spirit, dimmer in vision and harder in heart than she had ever done before.

<h1 style="text-align:center">6</h1>

ARDHALLOW WAS AFTERWARDS to maintain that no town its size could have been expected to cope with an orphan boy's disappearance on top of a murder and a suicide. Besides, there were mountains behind the town stretching all the way to Loch Fyne. It would have taken the whole Highland Division to make a thorough search, and they'd have been at it for months, long after the boy must have perished from exposure and hunger.

What could be done was done with good will and diligence. All roads leading out of the town were patrolled. Householders were asked to search their sheds and out-houses. Enquiries were made at the pier and on the ferries. Appeals for information were made on the radio. Shepherds were asked to look in bothies and deserted cottages. Tommy's housemates in the Home and class-mates at school were questioned. The two Homes he had been an inmate of previously were warned to be on the look-out for him.

True, it was admitted in private that if the boy had had a parent or any relative at all willing to make a great fuss then the search might have been that bit more diligent and would have gone on a little longer. But the result would have been the same.

Mrs Maxwell, during the first few days of the disappearance, telephoned the police several times a day. If she'd been his mother she couldn't have done more.

By the third day people had begun to say that if he wasn't found very soon then he'd never be found alive. One of those saying it was Mr Roger Falconer, Rector of the High School. Indeed, by the afternoon he'd said it to three members of his staff, and twice to his secretary.

Now within a year of retirement Mr Falconer had always staunchly claimed success only with normal, biddable, industrious, respectful, academically ambitious children. "I'm no miracle-worker," he would admit, with white-haired honesty. His school, like that in most small Scots towns, was thoroughly comprehensive in that it had to take in every child of secondary age in the district. It followed that among the eight hundred or so there were always in any year at least a dozen misfits with whom he could do nothing except belt them, which never succeeded, or send them away, which succeeded so well that the law had to be used to get them back again. That year's sharpest thorn in the flesh was Largie, so troublesome and un-teachable that his teachers were only too glad to throw him out of their rooms, so that Mr Falconer, making his rounds, would come upon him scribbling huge phalluses on the corridor walls or in the library looking earnestly at forbidden encyclopaedias. More than once, the head-master had just turned and crept away, leaving Largie as undisturbed as a tiger feeding, and as unredeemed.

Young Springburn had been no Largie, thank God. He had been reported by his form teacher, Miss Downie. Her complaint had been baffling. He had not said so, out of tact, but it had seemed to him that any boy who gave no trouble, was never disobedient and did his work reason-ably was a godsend to any school. That he was reticent to the point of muteness was surely an extra gain rather than a fault. A school with eight hundred like him would be a headmaster's paradise.

Mr Falconer had not got to know the boy. He could

not have pointed and said, "You, Springburn, come here," as he could so readily with Largie and his like. Indeed, it was the great bitterness of Mr Falconer's career that of the thousands of ordinary decent children who had passed through his hands he had got to know very few; whereas every rapscallion had been as close to him as a son or daughter.

When Springburn went missing, and the police called, Mr Falconer could not put a face to the name. He sent for Miss Downie who reminded him that she had mentioned young Tommy's peculiar taciturnity. Rather testily, he had remembered: it still seemed to him that in a school full of roarers Miss Downie had been too zealous in reporting one voluntary mute.

But neither he nor Miss Downie nor any of the boy's classmates were able to help the police. It turned out nobody knew anything about him: he might have been a ghost. Still, as the headmaster pointed out, he had been in the school only three months. A boy like that, who minded his own business and loved secrecy, could easily after five years be still unknown. Largie, he could have added but didn't, had made his mark the very first day, by demolishing the drinking fountain in the boys' lavatory.

All the same, Mr Falconer liked to look on himself as being *in loco parentis* to all his pupils. "I've got more children than the Sultan of Araby," he'd once quipped on the golf course. Therefore he worried a bit about Springburn and, that afternoon of the Tolmies' funeral, looked out of the window at the ferocious rain and hoped the silly little chap was at least in shelter somewhere.

An hour later, though, after an unsatisfactory conversation by telephone with an American mother who accused his "Scatch kids" of bullying her son Herman, a known pest, he was getting ready to enjoy a well-earned cigarette when there came a knock on his study door. Before he could shout "Come in" or "Go away", for sometimes Largie in passing gave the door a bang, it opened and in marched, God help him, a problem of the past that he thought he'd got rid of.

While at school Ann Plenderleith, sister of the exemplary Dora, had been as it were a Largie in reverse: where the latter was pure evil she had been almost as provokingly pure good. Not in Agnes Tolmie's Jehovah-will-get-you way, which any headmaster was bound partly at least to approve, but in a remember-what-Jesus-said way that might have been bearable if spoken with appropriate meekness, not uttered like threats. Agnes had been all for the thrashing of delinquents for their own good; Ann had been for the abolition of thrashing. She had wanted the school to be run on love not fear, though she'd said it so intemperately as to make everybody afraid. She had complained about teachers smoking and setting a bad example. If she hadn't been the daughter of the highest-paid minister in the town she'd have got her angelic wings clipped; which would have been a kindness, for look where her absurd flights had taken her, first to those demonstrations and then into a state of mental collapse.

Nervously he pushed his cigarettes back into the drawer. It was his room, his sanctum, and he could do whatever he pleased in it, but all the same he wouldn't have enjoyed his smoke scrutinised by that intense stare, which one teacher had likened to that of St Teresa, a lady, it seemed, who'd kissed the scabs of lepers.

He felt not only morally but physically naked. Yet over his good tweed suit he wore his academic gown, surely the most respectable garb in Christendom.

He wondered if he should make some excuse and slip into the outer office to ask Mrs Shieldhill to phone for the minister. Then he remembered Plenderleith at that very moment was probably handing over the souls of the two Tolmies to the Lord. If Ann proved difficult he could always send for Miss Greenloaning, her stepmother-to-be.

He wondered if her father knew she was out. She wore a red raincoat with red hat and Wellingtons to match. She didn't look a bit emotionally exhausted, which was how he'd heard her condition described.

"Well, Ann," he said, with magisterial cheerfulness, "this is a surprise. It's nice to see you out and about again. Not much of a day though for walking, eh?"

Did she know her father was conducting a funeral that afternoon? Had she been told about the murder? He had heard she was being kept in purdah.

"I was just passing," she said. "I thought I'd call in and see how Tommy Springburn was getting on."

Mr Falconer remembered she had been friendly with the boy before her illness; or rather she had plagued him with her unfortunate friendliness. He had no idea, however, that Springburn's unwillingness to speak to anyone had been attributed by her to the withdrawal of God. Had he been told that he would have laughed sturdily. In his experience children had lost all manner of things: school-books, dinner tickets, money, bicycles, articles of clothing, even brothers and sisters, but none had ever mislaid God.

"Oh yes," he said.

Then, hypnotised by those blue eyes, he spoke the truth. "Didn't you know, he's run away. Three days ago. They're still searching. Nobody knows what made him do it. Hope's running out, I'm afraid."

What if, in all innocence, in stupidity too all the same, he had as it were dropped a bomb into her mind which the doctors had just patched together? He waited for it to go off, though he wasn't sure what the signs would be. Mouth opening imbecilically? Clawing of the face? Screaming?

She continued to be very composed; reconciled seemed the better word, though what to he couldn't have said.

"Yes, I thought it must be that," she said.

"Seems he couldn't have been altogether right in the head. Never spoke to anybody. Worried us. We noticed he was peculiar of course, but what could we do?"

"Another thing," she said. "Is it true that Agnes Tolmie's father killed Luke Dilworth?"

This was a bigger bomb altogether.

"You'll have to ask your father that," he said.

"So it's true then. They've been hiding things from me, you know."

He wondered what fool had told her.

As if reading his thoughts, an easy trick according to most of his staff, she said, "Mr Stiegel called. He's the American chaplain."

"Oh him." Like Miss Breckinridge Mr Falconer didn't think much of a man of the cloth who wore very tight trousers of shepherd's tartan.

"He forgot father was at the funeral."

"Funny thing to forget."

"He told me."

"Well, I don't think he was supposed to."

He wondered what he could do or say to prevent her suffering a relapse. After all, the reason why his salary was double that of any other member of his staff was because he had twice their ability to handle children.

"Anyway, Ann," he said, with a grin, "when you're in Edinburgh at the university you'll not be bothering your head with Ardhallow's petty little affairs."

"I wonder how Agnes is taking it," she said.

"Well, wasn't she brought up to accept the will of the Lord? Like Jephtha's daughter you might say. Mind you, I don't know if you or I would call murder the will of the Lord exactly, but Agnes might. In that case, if you see what I mean, she might suffer it better than you or I would. At the same time, if her faith gave way, and God knows it's got some dunt, then she'd suffer all the more. If she recovers from this it'd be in a way a recommendation for religion. Though an atheist might say what her father did cancelled it out."

He had spoken too much, let his thoughts show too clearly. It was a fault that made staff meetings lengthy and inconclusive.

The period bell rang. In his mind he saw the children pouring out of rooms and along corridors. Some would drop crisp packets. Many would slouch with hands in pockets. Some would stop to chat with boy or girl friends, causing blockages and lateness. Some would aim gratuitous blows at cronies. Some might even sing the song that had been composed about the murder.

They would not be a credit to the school if, say, an H.M.I. happened to see them, but they were, thank God, natural. It wasn't often that Mr Falconer thanked God for the naturalness of children.

Ann rose. "I think I'll go and see Mrs Maxwell," she said. "I'd like to make sure they're searching for him as hard as they can."

He found it difficult to say just what sort of juvenile arrogance that was. He did what in his career he had done too infrequently: he stifled his professional wrath and said nothing.

"Good afternoon," said Ann, and left.

Greedily he took out a cigarette and lit it. He was afraid she'd come back or the American woman would phone again.

He stood up and looked out out of the window. Soon Ann appeared on the drive, in the swirling rain. Beyond her, in a mist of wetness, lay the town where a murderer was being buried. He remembered that he was almost sixty-five and according to statistics a teacher after that age could count on an average on only another eighteen months to live. He felt the cold clay being heaped on top of him.

Though he had nothing to say to her for the moment

he went into the office to look at Mrs Shieldhill. It was enough just to stare at her and nod, in homage to plain everyday brains at work on such sustainingly tedious tasks as attendance returns and requisition sheets.

PART FOUR

I

AFTER THE LONG wet cold raw murky winter, Ardhallow and district enjoyed, almost every year, a spell of keen dry sunny weather that went on, miraculously, day after day, for weeks. Elderly people, well happed up, shivered now for joy, not fear: life was still beautiful, death not so menacing. Children, sent on errands for such dull stuff as boot polish or soap powder, raced to and from the shops with yells and loups and hip-smitings of delight. Even the dustiest sparrow had a beak of silver.

Streets and houses, well washed after months of vigorous rain, were now polished by the bright abrasive wind. The whole town shone, including the gravestones in the cemetery, and the moss on the parapet of Sodger's Brig.

More than one panting overweight citizen, thinking really of himself, remarked to his wife what a pity it was that Edgar Oliphant hadn't been spared to enjoy this annual rejuvenation of the town he'd served so well. For the fat little lawyer, not long after the Tolmie murder, had taken a heart attack while standing on a low stool in his office, looking down on to the main street; he had died within minutes. He was cremated in Greenock. His place as Convenor of the County had been taken by a landward colonel.

There had been another death of note. Mrs Hossack, resourceful town councillor, amazed and shocked her col-

203

leagues by dying quietly of a brain haemorrhage. A native of Glasgow, she had been buried there.

The family from Glasgow who had bought Granny Brisbane's house with some natural misgivings were relieved to find that every blade of grass in the garden gleamed like new, and the stone slab at the back door on which the American's life blood had poured out, now, by this daily absolving sunshine, had its sinisterness removed, so that their four-year-old daughter could bounce her red ball on it and sing happily.

Mick the cat was never seen in the garden again, though blackbirds were.

The other house, along the road, was still empty; but with weather like this gilding it a purchaser could come along any day prepared to pay a good price. It was thought young Agnes would never live in it again.

At the High School Mr Falconer had long ago taken the name Tommy Springburn off his roll: though he had to hold on to the boy's Progress Card, there being no known educational authority to send it to. But this was too small a worry to be carried on to the golf course where the ball, however inadequately struck, glittered in the air as beautifully as a swallow's breast.

To the expatriate Americans it was like waking up after hibernation. Suddenly one morning there was this brightness and pellucidity of air, that turned even concrete lamp standards into columns of beauty; and it continued all day, and next day too, and the next, for weeks. Two of them not there to enjoy it were Burroughs and his buddy Steve; their stint over, they had gone back gratefully to the States. Returned too were the Rev. Harry Stiegel and family; not happily as it turned out, for Trixie in spite of his best contraceptive efforts was pregnant again, and resented it greatly. Chuck Nelson still remained; he had four months to go.

*   *   *

One morning of this gracious weather Robert Plenderleith spoke for the whole town. He stood at the window of his bedroom in the manse, in pyjamas of blue-and-white fine cotton, and gazing out at the splendid durable sunshine murmured something fervent aloud.

Behind him, still in bed, his wife Elizabeth, in a knee-length lilac nightdress of silk as sheer as it could be and still avoid transparency, asked him fondly what he had said.

"I was saying, my love, that this lovely weather, day after day, is like a benison."

She got up and barefooted, still smelling of last night's bridal scent, went over to him.

They had had their pick of the five bedrooms, for Ann was now a student in Edinburgh and Dora had moved into a flat of her own in another part of the town. They had chosen this one for reasons never spoken. The best and biggest bedroom looked down on to the loch and the *Perseus*; for that reason Robert did not care to use it. It had been where he'd slept with his first wife; that was reason enough for Elizabeth to pass it by. So here they were in this rather small one, with its outlook to the noble and neutral hills. It was embellished with some of Elizabeth's best pieces.

She embraced him with a fervour that would have given the late Edgar Oliphant cause to reflect, and the still living Mrs Crichton reason for disgust. It also, very slightly, embarrassed Robert; but she had decided not to heed that. The only check to her marital amorousness was one he did not know about and never would. This was a remark made by Bella the dishwasher and overheard by Elizabeth; to the effect that if Elizabeth wanted a child she would have to get a move on. It had of course been expressed more earthily.

Elizabeth wanted a child very much. Though there were many other ways of showing her faith in God, in Robert, and in Ardhallow itself, having a child and bringing it up to love her native town seemed to her the best. That Robert, whose younger child was now almost nineteen, was not just so hasty, was only natural and she did not blame him. It did mean, though, this present slight imbalance in their physical desire for each other.

"Of course, darling," she murmured, lovingly, "it *is* a benison. But please, please, don't question if we deserve it."

"No, my love."

So, grateful to the Lord, they stood, clasping each other, and looking into the far distance where the sun shone on stone as white as snow on Ben More, the mountain that dominated the hills round Glen Canach.

2

THAT VERY MORNING, while the Plenderleiths were feeling blessed at their bedroom window, Jimmy McKendrick, father of Hamish, red-haired ten-year-old terror of Miss Breckinridge's school, was patrolling those Glen Canach hills, on fire duty. Piece-bag on one shoulder and firebroom on the other, chewing a sprig of bog myrtle to keep off the desire for a smoke—"Py God, Chimmy, I'll have the palls off any man I catch smoking," Mr McColm had threatened—McKendrick strode jauntily from one look-out point to another.

In the exhilarating air he felt heroic, fit for that high country of golden eagles and glittering peaks. He even sang, though his wife Morag told him he shouldn't ever, not even on the hills, where he would scare the deer. Going through a grove of scrub birch he saw some big Judas lugs, and carefully pulled one off. He stowed it in his bag wrapped in withered bracken. He hoped it wouldn't smell his sandwiches. Hamish had asked him to get one for Miss Tolmie's collection of unusual plants.

One look-out point was the green hill known as the

Sithean, the Hill of the Fairies. There, lying on the grass, he commanded a view of a wide flat planted with thousands of five-year-old Norway spruces. A broad-bladed yellow grass also grew there in abundance, turning the plain into a sheet of gold and also a dangerous fire risk. "A fart could set it going," McColm had said gloomily. Grinning, McKendrick eased up and tested; and for a few moments got a fright, for in one part where the grass was yellowest, the breeze ruffling it made an effect like flames.

As he gazed, reassuring himself, he noticed some hoodie crows on top of a big rock. He supposed the carcase of a sheep was there, for some pushed in through the fences, or of a deer. Whatever it was must be all eaten, for the birds were in no squabble of greed; they sat on the rock peaceably. A fastidious man—if a single ant got into his meat paste he'd throw the whole sandwich away—McKendrick tried not to think of those blunt beaks at work, piking out the eyes first and then tearing at the juiciest parts of the intestines. If he had had a gun he would have shot them. Everybody hated hoodies.

When he got up to continue his patrol he made for the rock though it was well off his course. He was curious, he wanted to chase those scavengers that had no right to look as peaceful as doves, but above all he wanted to show that he was his own boss that bright morning, with no forester or foreman to tell him what to do or where to go.

As he approached, the crows rose and flapped off, in silence. He wasn't surprised to find he was right, the corpse or skeleton lying under the rock hadn't a scrap of meat left on it; but what more than surprised him, what made his red hair bristle and his knees so stiff that he could hardly creep forward, was that the arrangement of bones was neither sheep-like nor deer-like, and under them was neither wool nor hide, but remnants of clothing. On one bony foot was a shoe with holes in it through which the hoodies had got in at the flesh.

Telling the story that night to his wife, with Hamish listening big-eyed, McKendrick was to confess that what worried him most during those first few horrible moments was where the other shoe could be. He even looked for it among the small trees and grass round about.

Suddenly, as if he'd just heard an order roared by some boss far superior to forester or district officer even, he rushed off, with a dozen stumbles, towards the hut more than half a mile away where there was a telephone connection with McColm's office in the glen.

Many a pleasant half-hour filched from back-breaking work had McKendrick spent in that small hut, smoking and sheltering from rain, or calculating how much he'd made at piece-work draining. But this morning he kept the door open and stood as close to the sunshine as the cord let him.

McColm's voice burst into his ear in frantic spurts.

"What is it, Chimmy? For God's sake, don't tell me there's a fire."

"No, Mr McColm, there's no fire. It's worse."

The forester laughed. "You're a ploody choker, Chimmy." Then he grew stern. "You know the rule, Chimmy. Only essential messages."

"I don't know if you'll think this an essential message."

"Dammit, Chimmy, any man with a prain in his head would know what an essential message is."

"I've found a body."

"A pody? Do you mean a sheep's?"

"I'd hardly phone you to tell you I'd found a dead sheep. It's human. A child's, I would say. A boy's."

"You must have been on the Sithean, Chimmy. The fairies have addled your prains."

McKendrick felt peeved. It didn't need fairies to addle McColm's brains.

"On the Glenafiach flat," he said.

"Away up there, for God's sake? It must be a sheep's."

"Have you ever seen a sheep's skeleton with a shoe on its foot?"

"A shoe?"

"Aye, a shoe."

"Well, Chimmy, somepody could have stuck an old shoe on a sheep's foot for a choke. Some men as you well know have a funny sense of humour. No child's missing from the glen, you know that."

"Aye." McKendrick grunted with relief that among the children not missing was his Hamish.

Suddenly McColm began stammering with excitement.

"Py God, Chimmy, I've been thinking. There was that poy went missing from the Home in Ardhallow months pack."

McKendrick frowned: he didn't like to be proved slower on the uptake than a man from Jura.

"I thought of him," he muttered, not truthfully. "But it's all of twenty miles from Ardhallow. And Glenafiach's a long way up into the hill."

"Well, Chimmy, if it's not him it must pe a sheep."

"It's not a sheep."

"If I mind right it was a pig of a night too. This isn't a climate we've got, Chimmy, it's a ploody provocation. Here we're praying for rain, and not as much as would wet a hen's toe. When we can do without it down it comes fit to drown a whale."

"What d'you want me to do about this, Mr McColm? Shouldn't it be reported?"

"Don't you worry, Chimmy, I'll give the polis in Ardhallow a ring. If they're interested they can come and take a look. You chust carry on, Chimmy. We don't want a million skeletons, do we?"

Again McKendrick, with those bones in his head, was slow on the uptake.

"The trees, Chimmy man, the trees. Have you ever seen

a forest that's peen purnt? It would make you weep. Thousands and thousands of plack skeletons. Walk through them and you come out like a nigger. Off you go, Chimmy. I'll let you know later if it was chust a sheep."

3

MISS BRECKINRIDGE HEARD about the discovery on the hill from Mr McTeague, as he passed the school on his way home.

She was walking about the quiet playground, agitated but not sure by what, unless it was the day's long clarity. There was a fragrance of wood smoke. A curlew called. Much nearer a child sang, not for the beauty of the song but from sheer joy or fun. Patches of sunlight still lit up the highest hills, though the tops of the tall pines along the river were in darkness. Soon the stars would appear and blaze as they had done the previous nights. Why all this almost supernatural light? Something of importance was being revealed now, at this very moment, but she wasn't clear enough minded to see it.

McTeague's footsteps were slow and deliberate. She recognised him from them. He was a big slow-moving slow-thinking man whose two little boys Donald and Douglas had luckily in one way and unluckily in another taken after him: they had his placid good nature and not their mother's discontented sharpness, but also his slow wits and not her quick ones.

"Good evening, Mr McTeague," she called, through the thick hawthorn hedge.

He stopped. "Evening, Miss Breckinridge. You won't have heard yet?"

She went to where she could see him through a gap. On his face was a gravity given him by the high solitudes in which he had been working all day.

"Heard what, Mr McTeague?"

"What Jimmy McKendrick found."

"No, I didn't hear. What was it?"

He spoke slowly and solemnly. "The body of that boy that ran away from the Home in Ardhallow, months ago. Well, what was left of it. The hoodies had been busy, as you'd expect; and maybe a fox or two. Up on the Glenafiach flat. He'd likely come past your gate here, Miss Breckinridge. All our gates, you might say. It was a dark wet night, they tell me. Mr McColm says the polis think he might have been trying to contact Miss Tolmie; she knew him. She wasn't here that night, if you remember. But surely Glenafiach was far out of his way. You'd have thought it'd have been a lot easier just to lie down under the bridge—" in the still air they could hear the river—"or even in your shed there. It's a mystery right enough."

He waited but could think of nothing else to say. Neither could she. They listened to a child laughing in the village.

"Well, good night, Miss Breckinridge. Seems a pity such a thing should have happened in our glen. Well, it's been so peaceful here."

He touched his cap and walked slowly away.

She found herself profoundly affected. She was shaking all over. She felt like screaming.

"Mr McTeague," she called, as sanely as she could.

He stopped. "Aye?"

"They didn't just leave his remains up there, did they?"

"No, no. The polis took away what was left in a bag. Jimmy's built a wee cairn. Mr McColm's grumbling that folk will come to look at the spot and maybe set fire to the forest. But that's not likely. It's too far up. It's a long hard climb."

He waited. She could find nothing to say.

She listened to his steps dying away. Then, feeling weak, she went over to the tree stump and sat down, her fists clenched in her lap.

In her, increasing like a curlew's cry—there *was* a curlew

crying—was a desperation. Though there were none in sight people weren't far off. If she stood on the stump she could see the lights in the village. But even if the whole village came to the playground, and the whole town of Ardhallow, she would still feel impenetrably alone. No one could get close to her. Yet everybody must share this sense of guilt and inadequacy paining her like a fatal disease.

She thought of the boy, her victim.

Soaked, exhausted, hungry, feet blistered and back sore, as he walked past he must have noticed the light in her window: she seldom went to bed before midnight, often long after. Perhaps in his imagination he had seen her seated cosily by the fire. Yet he had not come through the gate, knocked on her door, and asked her for help. On the long walk from Ardhallow he had passed many doors, but it was her share of the failure that concerned her. Absolutely no exoneration or extenuation was allowed. She had failed, that was all. She had been too content with the store of humanity she had gathered; it hadn't been enough. If everybody's store was as meagre as hers, all the world's put together wouldn't be enough.

Perhaps it was because she was so desperate for hope, for a reason to be optimistic, that she thought of Agnes there, beyond the dark pines, happy mistress of Fern Cottage. What would Agnes the devout make of the boy's shameful death? She had emerged from the hell of murder, suicide and cancerous death undaunted, with her faith, it seemed, stronger than ever, too strong indeed for the liking of some of the village women. These had hinted to Miss Breckinridge that in their opinion Agnes was just a bit above herself: she had a way of talking to you as if you were beneath her. Why, even Lady Laird-Muscott, wife of the Conservator, when she had visited the glen some years back, hadn't been as lofty-minded. Perhaps Miss

Tolmie couldn't help it: it was delayed hysteria or something.

You'd think, they whispered, her father had done something marvellously good instead of murdering a man and killing himself. Also did you notice she was inclined to treat as a handmaiden her aunt who'd come to keep house for her? And as for her uncle left behind in Ardhallow with his rabbits she didn't seem to have as much consideration for him as she should.

In spite of all that, when asked if they thought Miss Tolmie was having a bad effect on their children they all replied that that was the strange thing, she was having a very good effect. On the alert for any attempt on her part to indoctrinate their children with the dreary side of religion, which after all had driven her father to commit murder, they had to admit they could see none.

Whenever the children spoke of Miss Tolmie, and they did it often, they laughed gleefully, as if at some joke only they could see. But in their laughter was a remarkable respect.

All the women were very willing to forgive Miss Tolmie her unconscious arrogance because of that joy she inspired in their children.

As for Miss Breckinridge herself, she had been having her own secret thoughts and fears about Agnes. She acknowledged the girl's courage, keenness and energy, but she hadn't yet been able to decide whether these admirable qualities were serving stupidity or the Lord. Agnes wasn't clever. At times she revealed a thickness of understanding that provoked the headmistress. Her knowledge of world affairs was sketchier and shallower than a teacher's should be, and her interest in them briefer. To that extent she was undeniably stupid.

As a good Presbyterian Miss Breckinridge did not believe in saints: all their visions to her were mere hallucinations. She did believe, though, that throughout history there had been women of superior moral force who had resolutely done good in evil times. Intellectually some of them had been as ordinary as Agnes. No doubt their like existed today. But that Agnes Tolmie was one Miss Breckinridge found it very difficult to believe.

After all, she was pregnant, nowadays conspicuously so; indeed, at the end of the week she was to start her six months' leave of absence. Her child would have no father. In what circumstances it had been conceived Miss Breckinridge had refused to find out either by asking or conjecturing. It was none of her business. But surely it disqualified Agnes and made her vulnerable.

All through the long winter Miss Breckinridge had waited, with foreboding, for Agnes to shed that enigmatic self-confidence like a flower its petals or a tree its leaves. She had been ready with pity and help, but she had not been needed. Agnes was a flower that had carried its petals throughout winter.

Would they be blighted at last by this chill wind from the hill, from the spot where the boy's body had been devoured by crows and foxes?

4

NEXT MORNING THE headmistress was in her most depressed, irritable mood for years. Usually as she stood on the school steps, greeting the children lined up in front of her, she saw in their young faces justification for hope that the eagerness and loving-kindness which was making them so beautiful would be retained into maturity. This morning it was the inevitable degeneration into adult selfishness, boredom and triviality that she foresaw.

They had all heard about the discovery Hamish's father had made. It seemed to her there was gloating in their eyes. They kept looking at Hamish. He basked in self-importance. He held something in his hand. They craned to see it.

Once before, when she had ordered him to show her what he was cherishing so reverently and so conceitedly in his fist, it had been only a bumble-bee, crushed almost to death. Its legs feebly moving had reminded her, grotesquely, of a new-born baby. In revulsion she had struck it out of his hand. He had been outraged, the rest of the children displeased.

Therefore this morning when she felt so irritable she ought to have ignored him. Better still, she ought to have handed over the marching-in to Agnes and gone back to the schoolhouse, to take a cup of tea and another two aspirins. But when she looked at Agnes and saw that smug holy smile and big brazen belly she was provoked beyond control.

She screamed to the children to stand still and keep quiet. Hamish she ordered to bring to her what was in his hand.

They were all astonished at her outburst. Some were frightened. One little girl, five years old, must have thought she was the one who'd caused offence: she burst into tears and ran across to take Agnes's hand.

Hamish stood his ground, shaking his head and tightening his fist. He looked behind to see that the way to the gate was clear. Whatever absurd treasure he had he was determined to flee rather than give it up.

"Do what you're told," screamed Miss Breckinridge.

He shook his head.

"It's nothing, Miss Breckinridge," called Mary McBride. "Only a button."

They all nodded. One or two plucked at buttons on their own clothing, and smiled.

"He says," cried Fiona McTaggart, "his dad got it off the dead boy."

215

Some laughed nervously. Others glanced up at the hill-tops already bright with sun.

"My dad found him," announced Hamish, proudly.

He took another peep at the wonder in his hand, and seemed to be satisfied; whoever might scoff this was a true relic.

"He says," said Angus McFarlane, "that it's got blood on it. But it's only rust."

"We think," said Mary, "it's just one of his own buttons he's pulled off. He's just showing off."

"His trousers'll fall down," cried Duncan Lamont.

They laughed.

With his free hand Hamish opened his jacket and pulled up his pullover to show that it was a belt which held up his trousers, not braces which needed buttons. It was elastic, red, white and blue, and its clasp was a silvery snake.

Miss Breckinridge tried to speak in a calm, authoritative voice.

"Whatever it is, Hamish, bring it here."

He took a step back.

"In our house," said Fiona, "we've got a big box with dozens of buttons just like that."

Others murmured that in their houses too were such boxes. One girl said that on the lid of her box was painted Ardhallow Pier.

Hamish got ready to run.

Miss Breckinridge felt faint. She wanted to sink down in front of them and weep. It would be a ridiculous ending to a career distinguished for dignity and common sense. She would be remembered for it all their lives.

She felt a hand on her arm. She turned. There was Agnes's provokingly wise smile.

"Let me talk to them," Agnes whispered.

The headmistress wanted to scream: "What can you do for them I can't? I've had more years than you've had

216

weeks dealing with children. I see them for what they are. I love them. You use them. I don't know how but you use them."

But why, with all that superiority, did she find herself unable to talk to them naturally and usefully? My father, she cried inwardly, never killed anything but the bullfinches stealing his blackcurrants. Yours killed a man. And you're going to have a child. Is it this which gives you, in their still primitive minds, a fascination? Do they think you will produce a miracle for them, or at any rate what they'll accept as a miracle? I never had a child laugh at me in all my life. Everything I've ever said to them has made sense.

"Look, Miss Breckinridge," said Agnes, "the hills are joyful."

Vaguely the headmistress remembered it as a quotation from the Bible. She tried to say, "Take care, Agnes," meaning, "Don't when their minds are greedy for mystery take advantage of it," but she was too ashamed.

She went inside and stood behind the door.

Agnes at once lifted the brass bell standing on the step and rang it merrily. She went on ringing it until the children, excited, began to cheer and laugh.

When she put it down again, with a last tinkle, there followed a silence any magician would have envied.

"Hamish, come here," she cried.

He went forward immediately.

"I wasn't being cheeky," he said. "I just thought she'd take it from me."

"You should have done what you were told, Hamish. I'm not pleased with you."

"Sorry, miss."

The others gasped at his humility, which they didn't trust. Miss Breckinridge gasped too and almost rushed out to grab him.

"May I see this button, Hamish?" asked Agnes.

"Sure, miss."

Reverently he held out his hand and opened it.

"It's just a button," the children murmured.

Agnes picked it up.

Some of them, as if embarrassed, glanced up at the sunlit joyful hills.

Miss Breckinridge looked up at her lonely tree on the crag. This day too, like yesterday, would not break down but would keep its promise. The thought heartened her strangely.

The children, she saw, had the same feeling of confidence, but not only in this one day, in the whole of life.

"Now, Hamish," said Agnes, briskly, "I want the truth. Where did you get this?"

"My dad gave it to me, miss," he cried, with explosions of earnestness. "Sure as God, miss. He picked it up off the grass. For good luck. The polis took the bones in a tattie bag. My dad helped them."

Little Sheila McColm, clutching her bag, the best in the school, wore the worried look which so often indicated that her answer, in arithmetic or anything else, would not quite make sense. Her lips moved. Perhaps she was whispering to herself that her father too had helped but had got no button. But then he was the boss of all their fathers, a man apart therefore, just as his house was apart.

They were still enjoying the mystery of the button. They were eager to hear what Miss Tolmie who was going to have a baby and whose father had killed a man would say about it.

Agnes bent down and gazed into Hamish's eyes.

"I don't think you're telling the truth, Hamish," she said. "This button hasn't been lying in snow and rain for months. Where did you get it?"

He hunched his shoulders, scowled, and clenched his fists. Miss Breckinridge wouldn't have been surprised if he'd let fly at Agnes's leg with his boot.

218

"I found it," he muttered, "in a drawer."

Some of them laughed but all approved of his confession. This did not keep them from looking disappointed and puzzled.

Miss Breckinridge was aware she had just watched a small miracle: Hamish McKendrick giving up a prestigious lie for the crestfallen truth.

"Thank you, Hamish," said Agnes "for telling us the truth."

He relaxed and looked pleased with himself again.

Agnes addressed the children.

"I knew the little boy," she said.

They nodded, eyes shining: the mystery was still alive, and proceeding.

Even so, truth had still to be told. "He wasn't very little," said Fiona. "He was at secondary school. He was older than us."

"That's true, Fiona. He was twelve. He was called Springburn, after the place in Glasgow where he was found when a baby, only a day or two old. So he was given that name."

One or two murmured their own names which were real names.

"So he never had any people," said Agnes.

"But, Miss Tolmie," said Mary McBride, "everybody must have people."

They all nodded, but some not too confidently. These were the five- and six-year-olds who weren't altogether sure where babies came from, in spite of Miss Tolmie's stomach so much bigger now than at Christmas.

"That's true, Mary. But he never knew who his were."

"Not even his mummy?" asked one of the five-year-olds, Betty McCartney.

"No, Betty, not even his mummy. So all his life he had to live in Homes, looked after by strangers."

"Were they cruel to him?" asked Fiona.

"No, Fiona, I'm sure they weren't."

"Why did he run away then?"

They nodded. The only time they had ever threatened to run away from home was when their parents had been unkind to them.

Miss Breckinridge wondered what she herself would have given as the reason. Because he was not quite sane, being unable to live in kinship with other people? It wasn't so rare a disease; everybody suffered from it, in varying degrees.

"My dad said," cried Angus McFarlane, "that he was looking for you, Miss Tolmie."

"No, Angus, he wasn't looking for me. He was looking for Jesus."

Miss Breckinridge was appalled: she felt as if the children had been exposed to a gross obscenity. So it *was* stupidity that inspired Agnes, and a kind not uncommon. God was made the excuse for avoiding responsibility and blame. Say you believed in Him and then consider yourself free to behave as selfishly as you liked. Say the boy was looking for God, or for Jesus if it was children you were trying to deceive, and then there was no need to worry about what he really had been looking for.

She would have rushed out and ordered Agnes to stop if she hadn't seen that the children didn't need her protection. They frowned, suspecting trickery. Looking for trout in burns or squirrels in trees made immediate sense for there was a good chance of finding them. Looking for Jesus was something that had to be explained and justified, for how would you know when you'd found Him?

"Well, he didn't find Him," said Duncan Lamont. "That's for sure."

"Why do you say that, Duncan?" asked Agnes, gaily.

"Because he died, didn't he?"

"Why didn't Jesus make the hoodies bring him food instead of eating him?" asked Angus.

"Like Elijah," added Fiona.

Miss Breckinridge glanced at her watch. Twenty minutes had been wasted already. The arithmetic lessons should have begun.

"Why didn't He, if He could?" asked Mary.

"Why should He, Mary? Tommy had come all that way in the dark and rain because he thought nobody really wanted him, in the way your fathers and mothers want you. So God thought, you see, that He'd take him Himself. Isn't it wonderful to know that when nobody else really wants you the Lord is sure to?"

Miss Breckinridge trembled at the speciousness of that reply, which surely begged the whole question. To her alarm it seemed to satisfy the children.

They marched past her into the school, singing joyously "What a friend we have in Jesus", and smiling forgivingly at her for having keeked out at them.

She realised she ought not to be alarmed, instead should be uplifted. Was she not a Christian herself, committed to a belief in God and in His love for His creatures?

Agnes was smiling at her. "It's all right, Miss Breckinridge," she said.

Annoyed that her subordinate should have the impudence to comfort her, she also felt, as she heard the children still singing the hymn, a bit cheekily now, that, in spite of everything, including her own doubts and her present irritation, it *was* all right.